My name is Callum Ormond.
I am sixteen
and I am a hunted fugitive ....

CONSPIRACY 365

BOOK NINE: SEPTEMBER

To Mathieu and Rory

Scholastic Australia
345 Pacific Highway
Lindfield NSW 2070
An imprint of Scholastic Australia Pty Limited
(ABN 11 000 614 577)
PO Box 579
Gosford NSW 2250
www.scholastic.com.au

Part of the Scholastic Group
Sydney • Auckland • New York • Toronto • London • Mexico City
• New Delhi • Hong Kong • Buenos Aires • Puerto Rico

First published by Scholastic Australia in 2010.
Text copyright © Gabrielle Lord, 2010.
Illustrations by Rebecca Young.
Illustrations copyright © Scholastic Australia, 2010.
Graphics by Nicole Leary.
Cover copyright © Scholastic Australia, 2010.
Cover design by Natalie Winter.
Cover photography: boy by Wendell Levi Teodoro (www.zeduce.
org) © Scholastic Australia 2010; close-up of boy's face by Michael
Bagnall © Scholastic Australia 2010; knife with blood © Anyka/
Shutterstock; truck tyre and red dirt © Diego Cervo/Shutterstock.

National Library of Australia Cataloguing-in-Publication entry:
Lord, Gabrielle, 1946-
  Conspiracy 365: September / Gabrielle Lord.
  ISBN 978-1-74169-321-8 (pbk.)
A823.3

ISBN-13:978-93-5103-683-8

Reprinted by Scholastic India Pvt. Ltd., August 2015

Printed at Shivam Offset Press, New Delhi.

CONSPIRACY 365

BOOK NINE: SEPTEMBER

GABRIELLE LORD

SCHOLASTIC
SYDNEY AUCKLAND NEW YORK TORONTO LONDON
NEW DELHI HONG KONG PUERTO RICO

PREVIOUSLY ...

1 AUGUST

I've been buried alive in a coffin. I can hardly move and the air is running out, fast. Boges and Winter use my mobile signal to track my position, but when they reach the cemetery they're confronted with a dozen fresh graves. Time's running out and they have no idea where to start digging.

2 AUGUST

I wake up in hospital and realise my hands are tied—I'm trapped in police custody! Turns out Boges and Winter had to call the authorities for help . . . to save my life. I'm questioned by Senior Sergeant Dorian McGrath about Gabbi—she's been kidnapped and I'm their prime suspect!

6 AUGUST

Mum and Rafe show up, begging me to tell them where Gabbi is. I can't believe they think I'm responsible. Later I find out the cops will be moving me from the hospital to a remand centre in the morning. Now is my last chance of escape. I use a broken scalpel blade to release my hands and I decide to flee through a ceiling panel.

7 AUGUST

Outside, security guards and cops are everywhere. I'm quickly spotted and chased. An ambulance skids into my path and a paramedic shoves me inside. Ex-detective Nelson Sharkey has come to my rescue. He finds a safe place to drop me off, and leaves me his card.

I'm surprised to find Boges at Winter's place. The three of us go over the night I was buried alive, and discuss how my DNA came to be at the scene of Gabbi's kidnapping. Do I have a twin, and could he be involved? Winter and I reveal our recurring nightmares—mine with the toy dog, and Winter's featuring sparrows, just like her tattoo.

18 AUGUST

Sharkey sets up a meeting for me with an underworld contact—Ma Little. She agrees to pass on a message for me to Gabbi's kidnappers.

22 AUGUST

I meet up with Griff Kirby who has promised me info about Gabbi. I'm shocked to find out he is Ma Little's nephew! We visit Dr Leporello—a police informant and expert in funghi—who gives me a number to call. As Griff and I are leaving, riot police jump out of a van and pounce! Sharkey comes to my rescue again, and I call the kidnapper's number and leave a message offering myself and what I know, in exchange for Gabbi's release.

I spot the 'No Psycho' tagger again and realise he's my double! I chase him all the way to his apartment. After he leaps out the window I lose him. Back in his room I discover his name is Ryan Spencer. On his shelf is the white toy dog from my nightmares!

27 AUGUST

When following Sumo I catch him buying something with 'Nutrition. Balanced formula. Intravenous', written on it. Oriana must have my coma-stricken sister! Sumo heads out of the city with the package. Is Gabbi being held out of town?

29 AUGUST

I get a call from the kidnappers telling me to meet them in a town called Billabong at nine pm on 31 August. Winter, Boges and I meet up with Sharkey to plan a doublecross.

31 AUGUST

Winter and I go to Billabong and wait by Spindrift River Bridge. When the kidnappers arrive I insist on seeing Gabbi before handing myself and my information over. I see her cocooned in a sleeping-bag. Sharkey's car suddenly speeds onto the bridge and he and Boges jump out to attack the kidnappers. During the fight, one of the guys picks up Gabbi and throws her off the side of the bridge. She tumbles into the raging water below. I dive in after her, frantically searching the river. How can she—in her unconscious state—fight for survival?

I finally find the sleeping bag, empty. Gabbi has been washed away. I've lost the Ormond Jewel, the Riddle and now my sister's life.

1 SEPTEMBER

122 days to go . . .

Spindrift River

12:00 am

Shivering, my fingers useless and numb, I staggered back to the stony bank near the bridge, and collapsed.

A blurry glaze fell over my eyes as I stared hopelessly across the dark river.

I was in shock. I'd lost my sister.

I'd lost her.

In my desperate searching for Gabbi, I'd completely forgotten about the kidnappers and my friends. I looked up to the bridge for a sign of movement, but could see nothing. It was like I was the only being in the world right now, sitting alone on the side of a savage river that had just stolen my little sister from me.

I turned back to the water.

Something suddenly caught my eye. Something

was stuck in the shadowy branches on the other side of the river.

Was something there or was my mind playing tricks on me? Creating shapes out of scattered moonlight and crooked driftwood? I rubbed my eyes and squinted through the darkness.

A gush of hope jolted through me—I was sure it was a figure! Half submerged and floating near the opposite bank! Could it be Gabbi, washed up and entangled in weeds on the riverbank? Could she still be alive?

I threw myself back into the freezing water and forced the burning muscles in my legs to kick, swimming diagonally through the current, trying to stop it from dragging me away downstream.

As I got closer, I became convinced it was Gabbi. The outline became more and more familiar with every frantic second. She could be alive, I repeated in my head. She could be alive.

The current was set on stopping me from reaching her. It pulled on me with all its might, but I pushed myself beyond my limits and forged ahead.

The water grew calmer, shielded from the rushing current by a narrow headland that acted like the wall of a dam. I was almost there. I thrashed over and finally I climbed to my feet in the shallow water.

I squinted and stared at the figure as I reached

for it. What I'd imagined was there—my sister—all of a sudden disappeared right in front of me. Her image was replaced by a lifeless mass of nothing.

I stopped short and screamed with frustration and fury, smashing the water with my fists. The snagged figure was nothing but some plastic sheeting, stretched into a grotesque scarecrow shape that from the other side of the river had looked like a small person.

It had all been wishful thinking. There was no way she could have still been alive.

I crawled up the bank once more, too drained to swear, and too wrecked to cry.

12:21 am

A brief thought of Mum swirled into my consciousness. She'd be devastated. This would mean the end for her. She wouldn't be able to go on without Gab. And she'd think that her own son had killed her daughter—that I escaped from the hospital to finish the job.

Like a wounded animal, I crawled further up the riverbank until I found a flat area.

I was numb, frozen, and half dead with exhaustion.

1:03 am

Crazy dreams whirled through my head. I

imagined Gabbi kneeling beside me, healthy and well. I imagined turning to her and saying, 'I saw you fall into the river. I went after you, but it was so hard to find you. The water was so cold and black and the current was impossibly strong. Please, forgive me, Gabs. I couldn't save you.'

Then my surroundings seemed to transform and we were back at Treachery Bay, mucking around in the tinny.

A storm was brewing. Gabbi was frightened. 'I shouldn't have brought you out here,' I say to her. 'I'm sorry.'

'Cal,' is all she says back to me.

'Cal,' she says again, in a haunting, distant voice.

Something powerful was suddenly shaking me. Had I fallen back in the river? Was I being bashed along by the current?

'Cal, wake up!' came Gabbi's sweet voice once more.

In my dream, she was shaking me by the shoulder. Wonderful warmth flowed through my body, waking up my frozen arms and legs, sending a tingling sensation to my fingers and toes.

For a moment, I let the good feelings run all over me. It felt like the storm at Treachery Bay had passed and the sun had come out and my sister and I were sitting in warm light.

The dreamlike vision of Gabbi was leaving me. Reality started hitting home, but I didn't want to wake up and open my eyes. That would mean facing the truth.

The truth that Gabbi was dead. That I hadn't been able to save her. That I was lying sodden on the banks of Spindrift River, with Gabbi gone forever, because of me. I had failed to protect her.

'Cal!'

I opened my eyes. A black shadow loomed over me.

Someone really was sitting beside me, shaking me.

I blinked.

The dream figure of Gabbi was still there.

Was this like the dream I had in the caravan when Great-uncle Bartholomew appeared to me, telling me that everything was going to be all right?

He'd lied. Nothing was all right. Everything was worse than I could ever have imagined. My sister was dead, and now I was seeing things.

I shook my head to clear the crazy whirlpool of images in my mind, but the figure from my dream was still there.

'Cal!'

Gabbi?

'Cal, what's happened?'

Gabbi?

'Cal, why won't you speak to me?'

Was I going crazy? Had my mind finally snapped completely?

'Gabbi?' I asked, squinting at the shape above me.

'It's me, Cal, what's going on? Why are we here?' Gabbi's voice was weak and slurred.

It was no hallucination. I was looking straight into my sister's face, and her small hand was clutching mine, gently squeezing it.

'Gabbi?'

'Yes, Cal, what's wrong with you?'

'Gabbi, it's really you! You're OK!' I reached for her, grabbing her cheeks with my hands, shocked to feel her soft skin and fair hair against me.

'Ouch, Cal, what are you trying to do?' she said, wriggling away from me.

'I'm sorry,' I cried, 'I'm just so happy to see you! And hear your voice! I can't believe you're alive!'

I stared at her. Her face had lost its childhood chubbiness, and by the moon's weak light she looked older. But it was Gabbi—alive! Kneeling beside me, confused and shivering!

'What are you talking about? I don't understand,' she said, looking around, her voice not much more than a whisper. 'Why are we here?

What are we doing here? It's really dark. I'm scared, Cal. Let's go home. *Please?*'

I grabbed her in my arms and held her tighter than ever before. If only I could take her home, I thought. If only I could just wrap her up in something warm, call Mum and then all of us could go home together . . .

'It's OK,' I whispered in her ear. 'Everything's going to be OK. I promise.'

I kept hugging her tight, trying to warm her up, trying to comfort her.

We clung onto each other and, gradually, her shivering eased. I pulled back and looked at her again. Her hair was flat and sleek on her head so that she looked like some little water creature. 'I'll get you home safe,' I promised.

'But I still don't know what's happening. Where are we?' she asked again. 'How come we went swimming in this river? In the middle of the night? How come I feel so . . . confused?'

'We didn't actually go swimming . . .' I started to say, but then stopped myself. I could see Gabbi was too dazed to understand right now. I could tell her everything later. It was just so good to have her here with me, alive, to know that she was OK. I pushed some wet hair back from her face, then grabbed her in a bear hug again. I had missed her so much.

'I thought I was back in the surf at Treachery Bay, being dumped,' she said as I let her go. 'I just kicked out and started swimming. I was stuck in some kind of bag or something.'

'You were in a sleeping-bag,' I said.

'Huh?'

'Let's get you warm,' I said, through my chattering teeth. I glanced around us, looking again for a sign of Boges, Winter or Sharkey. Or the kidnappers. 'We have to move.'

1:13 am

'C'mon, Gabbi,' I said, helping her up. We weren't out of danger yet. I had to check our surroundings. I had to find out what had happened to my friends. And I knew that the criminals could still be in the area.

Gabbi stumbled and fell to her knees.

I bent over to pick her up and was met with a wet, teary face. 'Cal, what's wrong with me?' she whimpered between sobs. 'My legs feel like jelly and I still have no idea how we got here!'

I took her face between my hands. 'You'll just have to trust me for a minute,' I said. 'I'll answer all your questions as best I can a little later, but right now we have to move. I have to check out some things. OK?'

She looked at me hopefully.

'OK?' I repeated. 'You can trust me, can't you?'

'OK,' she said, grabbing onto my arm to steady herself.

'Hop on,' I said, before pulling her up onto my back.

1:51 am

When we'd reached a high rocky outcrop, I stopped and let Gabbi slide off my back. I sat her on the grass and told her to wait while I looked down at the Spindrift River Bridge, from a spot just a metre or so away.

The lights that lined the bridge below were flickering on and off, swinging in the wind. There were still no signs of Boges, Winter, Sharkey or the kidnappers. The bridge was empty. Not a car was in sight.

I knew the kidnappers could still be in the area, hunting me. The thought of them being out there, lurking somewhere in the dark, was making me really nervous.

I turned to Gabbi and lifted her onto my back again.

Just as she looped her arms around my neck, I heard the sound of someone stealthily picking their way through the scrub. Immediately I started creeping backwards.

In the dim moonlight, I could just make out

the figure coming our way, head down, moving towards us.

I spotted a boulder and quickly lowered Gabbi behind it. I signalled to her that she should stay still, and placed my finger over my lips, hushing her before she could ask any questions. 'Don't come out till I tell you it's OK,' I whispered.

I flattened myself against the front of the rock, peering ahead. I was a metre or so higher than the intruder, so I had the advantage.

Whoever it was must have been heading this way to make use of the higher ground too, intending to look around, survey the land, just the way I had. I needed to take action before they walked straight into us. No way was I going to risk losing Gabbi now!

I sunk down and my hand closed around a fist-sized rock. The figure approached, broad-shouldered, but not very tall. As the figure came within two metres of me, I dropped on top of him, crashing us both to the ground, the rock raised in my right hand ready to crack it down if I needed to.

'What do you think you're doing?! It's me!'

I caught a whiff of the familiar perfume.

'Winter?'

She rolled me over and stared down into my face. Some of her hair slipped out of the black beanie she was wearing and onto my cheek. The beanie belonged to Boges. I didn't know where the leather jacket she was wearing had come from.

I realised I was still clutching the rock in my hand. I let it fall.

'I had no idea it was you. I saw the shape of the leather jacket and thought it was a guy. Maybe one of the kidnappers. I didn't get a good look at either of them. Are you OK? Are Boges and Sharkey OK?'

'I'm fine, they're fine!' she gushed. 'Thank goodness you're alive! Boges and I have been searching up and down the banks. We'd just about given up! We were going out of our minds!'

She fell on me again and hugged me tight. Her hair was damp on my neck.

'This is Nelson's,' she explained as she sat back up, pulling at the collar of the leather jacket. 'He had it in the back of his car. My clothes got soaked when I went in after you.'

'You came in after me?'

'I had to. Boges couldn't leave Nelson. He'd been injured in the fight and was bleeding badly. I didn't even think about it. I just dived in.'

'You crazy girl,' I said, amazed she was so brave, and secretly stoked that she'd dived into Spindrift River because of me. 'You could have drowned.'

'*You* could have drowned,' she repeated back to me, with a suddenly solemn tone. 'That river was impossible. It swept me along like I was a twig, and it was only good luck that I managed to grab onto some willow branches hanging over the river. You must remember that, Cal,' she said very seriously. 'The river was too strong for anyone. You couldn't have saved Gabbi. Nobody could have.'

'But, Winter—' I began, before being interrupted.

'Cal? Are you OK?' Gabbi's voice called out from the darkness.

Winter's eyes opened wide. Surprise, joy and relief shone on her face, even though much of her was in shadow. Without words, her eyes seemed to ask me, *Is it really her?*

I nodded.

'I'm fine, Gab,' I called back. 'Just wait there for me, OK?'

'OK,' she agreed.

Winter leaned in close to me. 'She's alive?' she whispered.

I nodded my head again and grinned. 'She made it. I don't know how she survived the fall, but she made it!'

'And she's awake!' Winter cried.

Winter leaped up and pulled me off the ground

with surprising strength. She started dancing me around in circles.

'Boges!' she shouted into the sky. 'I found him! He's right here! With Gabbi! They're both alive!'

My little sister crawled out of her hiding place and knelt there staring at the two of us, her eyes huge in her pale face, looking as if she was about to cry.

'Who's that?' she whispered to me. 'What is she talking about?' she asked.

'It's OK, Gab. Winter's here to help. She's our friend,' I said.

4:21 am

We sat around a warm campfire defrosting our fingers and toes, while our clothes steamed on tree branches near Nelson Sharkey's car. Boges had returned my backpack so I was able to change into dry clothes.

Sharkey was recovering from his injuries. Boges had patched him up pretty well. They assured me the kidnappers were long gone. 'What would they stick around for?' Sharkey had said to me. 'As far as they know there's nothing left here for them to take.'

The pre-dawn chorus of birds trilled, fussed and squabbled around us in the trees.

Even though I'd had no sleep and felt totally

trashed, I wanted to sing with those birds. Gabbi was safe, Gabbi was with me. My friends were here, Boges and Winter. Winter had dived into the flooded Spindrift River to save me.

The leather jacket was now wrapped around Gabbi who was snuggled up to me, with Boges close on her other side. She was napping while Boges filled me in on what had happened after I leaped into the river, chasing after my fast-vanishing little sister. In front of us, the small fire glowed.

'After you jumped, one of them was really getting stuck into Sharkey, while the other one—the one who threw Gabbi off the bridge—ran back to the car. Before I knew it, Winter had dived into the river, after *you*. That girl is nuts. Then I yelled out that a cop car was coming, and that made both of the kidnappers abandon the scene real fast.'

'Leaving Boges free to help me out,' said Sharkey, indicating a bandaged arm. 'I think I nicked my radial artery in that struggle. The guy had a knife. It's a long time since I've had to do any hand-to-hand combat,' he admitted with a shrug. 'I'm a little out of practice.'

'We watched them drive away,' Boges continued. 'I think the kidnappers just wanted to get out of there really fast. They took what they came for and had no need for your sister any more. They thought they'd rid themselves of you too, dude.'

'Wishful thinking,' I said.

Boges softly ruffled Gabbi's drying hair—she was curled up in his lap.

'How good is this?' said Sharkey. 'To have your sister back.' From the way he was looking at me I could tell his words were about to take a more serious tone. 'Enjoy it while you can, Cal. You know we're not going to be able to stay here with her for long. We're going to have to alert the authorities. She needs to be checked over by medical staff. And your mum and your uncle need to know she's safe.'

I nodded, sadly.

'She must be really tired,' said Boges. 'Poor thing.'

'No, I'm not,' came her muffled voice. She lifted her head. 'I feel like I've been asleep for days.' She rubbed her eyes and looked around at the four of us. 'Who had a knife? How come I can't stay with you?' Her pale face scrunched up and I could see she was trying hard not to cry. She looked from Boges to me, and back to Boges again. She squinted hard at him and reached for the short, brown fuzz on top of his head. 'Where did all your hair go?'

4:42 am

I knew when Gabbi was trying to be brave and right this minute she was doing it as hard as she could. I tightened my arm around her, trying to work out how to begin to explain everything to her.

Out of the corner of my eye, I saw Winter beckon to Sharkey and Boges, calling them away from us so we could have some quiet time together—just Gabbi and me. The three of them wandered off and stood in a circle a few metres away, chatting softly.

'Tell me what you remember, Gab,' I said. 'Start with what happened tonight, if you can. What do you remember about being in the river?'

'Well,' she began, 'I was in the water and it was freezing. I know it doesn't make sense, but I don't know how I got there—I was just suddenly . . . in the water.'

'It's OK,' I said. 'It doesn't need to make sense. Anything you say is OK.'

'I thought I was dreaming that I was being carried out on a rip in Treachery Bay. I was so scared. I felt trapped in something. I didn't know what was happening. Everything was mushy in my mind. But then I realised it was night and I wasn't at a beach. And it wasn't a dream—it was real. The water really was rushing me along!'

'It's OK, Gab, you're safe now. Keep going.'

'I was stuck in something, a sleeping-bag? I couldn't breathe. Somehow I wriggled out of it and then I collided with this log that was sticking out over the water. After a few seconds of scrambling to get my head above water, I used the branches to pull myself up and onto the bank. I was really scared. It was dark and I was wet and I didn't know where I was. I was crying out but no-one could hear me. I saw some lights in the distance, so I just started heading that way. I started walking back along the river-bank but it was really weird—I kept falling over like my legs had gone to sleep. They were shaky and tingly like I had pins and needles, but it wasn't that. My legs just wouldn't work properly. I kept stumbling and falling over like a little baby. But then one time I fell over and that's when I found you!'

Gabbi had reached the limit of her bravery. I felt her small body heaving as she started crying, and I squeezed her tight.

She looked up again, her face streaked with tears. 'I thought you were dead, Cal,' she wailed. 'You were just lying there. You were so cold. I was trying to wake you up but you wouldn't answer me!'

'It's OK, I'm here now.'

I decided on trying to tell her the truth of the situation, even though it was horrible. After what she'd been through, Gabbi deserved that.

'Gab, what do you remember happening before you fell into the river? I know you don't know how you fell in the river, but do you remember anything happening before that? Like, at home or at school?'

The puzzled look on her face deepened. 'What do you mean? I remember everything! I'm about to start Year 3 with Miss McCormack. Dad died. Last year. Why are you asking me that?'

I wondered how I was going to break the news about the months she'd lost in a coma.

'That's right,' I said. 'Just keep telling me anything you remember. What you remember happening before you ended up in the river. Then I'll explain what I can to you. OK?'

'I don't know! I don't know what else to tell you!'

'Just take a moment and think about it. Maybe something will come back.'

Gabbi took a deep breath.

She looked agitated and afraid as flickers of memories seemed to come back to her.

'I remember!' she said before speaking really quickly. 'I was upstairs in my room, texting Ashley on Mum's old phone, and then I heard some really loud noises downstairs. Yep, that's right. At first I thought it was you, so I called out. I called out for Uncle Rafe, too, but nobody answered me. Mum had gone shopping, so I knew she wasn't there. Then I heard these strange voices. I got really scared, thinking about the people who broke into our house last week.'

'Last week?'

'Well, *two* weeks ago, whatever. I thought it could have been them.'

Two weeks ago? The break-in, back home, was months ago!

'I was so scared,' Gabbi continued, 'I was even going to call the police! Then I heard these loud bangs and the strange voices got louder and I didn't know what to do! I was running to my wardrobe to hide when *bam!* Someone whacked me from behind! When that happens in cartoons, you see stars. But I didn't see any stars.'

Anger surged through me.

'Next thing I know,' explained Gabbi, 'I think I'm caught in a rip in Treachery Bay . . . except it wasn't the bay, it was this river here.'

In the flickering firelight, Gabbi's face was frightened and puzzled. She had lost the last eight months! She'd gone from that afternoon in January—when she was attacked and I found her slumped on the ground, not breathing—to this day, right now on the riverbank near Spindrift River Bridge.

'Why are you looking at me like that, Cal?'

I realised now that Gabbi would not be able to help me clear my name.

'Gab,' I said, 'they reckon I attacked you.'

'*You*?! But that's crazy!'

'Mum said you were yelling out my name when the ambulance came to get you.'

'I must have been scared for you! Scared they were gonna hurt you too. I think it was you they were after! I was trying to warn you!'

'Me? They were after *me*? What makes you say that?'

'I don't know! I don't remember! Maybe I heard them say something about you. I don't know.'

Gabbi was shaking her head, frustrated with herself for not remembering everything properly.

'I think I must have been awake for a second after I got hit. I didn't know where you were. I must have been trying to warn you before it all went black again. I don't know what happened. I didn't want them to get you.'

Boges, Winter and Sharkey had rejoined us. I looked across at Boges. He was nodding to me as if to say that was why Mum and Rafe thought I was the guilty party. That, and the fact that my fingerprints were on the gun that shot Rafe.

'They didn't get me, Gabbi. And,' I added, cautiously, 'it didn't actually happen last night. It happened a while ago. A *long* while ago.'

'How long?'

'You've been unconscious—in a coma—from the head injuries.'

'Huh?' Instinctively, Gabbi put her hand up to the back of her head. 'But I don't even have a lump! There's nothing there!'

'That's because you were hit almost eight months ago . . .'

'What? What do you mean, eight months?'

'Look,' I said, pulling my mobile out and showing the screen to her.

She read it out slowly. 'The first of September? But . . . how could I walk upstairs to my room one day,' she said, 'and then wake up in a river eight months later? Ashley will never believe me.' She grabbed my arm, tears welling up in her eyes again. 'Oh, no! That means I've missed almost a year of school! I'll have to repeat Year 3!'

'After a while it won't feel so weird. And you'll catch up at school really quickly. You're really smart, remember that?' I said with a playful nudge. 'You might even find that some memories of what happened to you will come back,' I added, thinking of something Boges had told me about memory loss and comas. 'Like where you've been, and who was looking after you.'

5:36 am

It took quite a while, but Gabbi finally started taking in what I was saying. I didn't want to freak her out too much, so was careful about what I said. I eased her into the current family situation and about my life on the run. I told her that she was now living with Mum at Rafe's house, and how happy they'd both be to find out she was all right and would be able to come home to them.

I didn't tell her about the time they almost switched off her life-support system, thinking she was never going to wake up. That would have been too much for anyone to take.

As dawn broke over the mountains in the distance, I had to tell her my side of the story—of how I'd been on the run, desperately trying to understand the mystery Dad had begun to uncover. Gabbi kept quiet through most of it, shaking her head in disbelief as I spoke.

'There is some huge secret attached to our family,' I said, 'that affects the first-born son in each generation.'

'That's you,' Gabbi pointed out.

'That's me. And I have to find out what it

means. I know that it's dangerous, so the stakes are high. Boges and Winter have both been helping me. And now Nelson Sharkey, too.' I put my arm more firmly around my little sister. 'He's an ex-detective. But you mustn't tell anyone anything I've told you. You have to keep it secret. It's too dangerous if you let on you know anything, OK? I'm afraid you can't even tell anyone—not Mum, not Rafe—that you've seen me.'

'But you saved me!'

'Gabbi Ormond,' I said very seriously. 'Please promise me you won't say anything.'

'Because of the police?'

'That's right. If I'm arrested, I'll never be able to clear my name and track down the Dangerous Mystery of the Ormonds. No-one can know where I am. You must pretend you know nothing, OK?'

'Cross my heart,' she said. 'I would never, ever dob on you.'

We linked pinkie-fingers and agreed to secrecy.

'I know. Thanks Gab.'

After telling her a bit about Winter, of how she'd saved my life once, Gabbi stared at her wide-eyed.

Winter gave Gabbi one of her rare smiles and Gabbi managed a smile of her own. That pink candle, I thought, remembering how it had glowed for Gabbi on Winter's desk, would not need lighting ever again.

'Bits seem to be flashing through my mind now,' Gabbi said, her eyes searching mine. 'I think I had some really strange dreams. Freaky. Really scary.'

'Tell us about them,' I said.

'This will sound weird, but I thought there was a woman. A really scary woman with red hair piled up on her head. And purple sunglasses.'

I was suddenly very alert. *Red hair. Purple sunglasses.* At some stage, Gabbi must have briefly regained consciousness and been aware somehow of Oriana de la Force! Oriana was definitely behind the kidnapping! Even though she already had the Ormond Riddle *and* the Ormond Jewel—the two precious parts of the double-key code—she had still wanted more.

Boges, Winter and Sharkey were leaning in, listening intently.

'Gab,' I said, leaning closer to her. 'I think that might have been real—not a dream. See, some stuff is coming back to you. That red-head is a real person. Can you tell me any more about her?'

'I don't think so,' she said, shaking her head. 'I feel like she was bossing these men around. But I think I was dreaming that, because I also felt like Uncle Rafe was there, protecting me.'

'Well that's good to hear,' I said. 'Even if it was only a dream.'

6:21 am

I promised Gabbi that I was well on my way to clearing my name so that I could come home and be with her really soon.

'I'm going to help you,' Gabbi announced solemnly, sitting back on her heels, her face very serious. 'I know I can't say anything to anyone, but somehow I'm going to help you.'

'Of course you are,' said Winter, leaning over to hold Gabbi's hand.

'Gab, when you're fit and strong, what would you think about being an undercover detective for me?' I asked.

'You can count on me,' she said with a grin.

'I'm sorry to say it, guys, but it's time we got going,' announced Sharkey, rearranging his bandaged arm. 'I can still drive, in spite of this.'

'So what's the plan?' asked Boges. 'We need a safe place to leave Gabbi.'

Gabbi looked at Boges nervously, biting her lower lip.

'There's a regional police station about forty kilometres from Billabong,' said Sharkey. 'Open all hours. We could drop Gabbi off there. Or near there—we don't want to bring our car in too close. Don't want to be identified and linked to her return.'

'Maybe if you park the car a few blocks away, I can walk her up,' suggested Winter, taking Gabbi's hand. 'Not to the door, of course, but I can take her as close as possible, and then I'll run for cover and meet up with you further down the road?'

'Good idea, Winter,' said Sharkey. He turned to Gab, who was looking more and more nervous by the second. 'Don't worry, sweetie, you'll be safe there. They'll take great care of you, and they'll have your mum and uncle over in two shakes of a lamb's tail. They'll also want to know how you got there. You can tell them a kind stranger dropped you off.'

'I guess that isn't really a lie,' said Gabbi slowly. 'You were a stranger, until just now. And I can tell you are both kind,' she said to Sharkey and Winter.

My sister looked up at me. Her lower lip was quivering.

'I know you said it's too dangerous, but isn't there some way you can come home with me, Cal?' she pleaded. 'You're my brother! Can't we just tell them it wasn't you who hurt me? *I* know that. I'll just tell them. We can explain every-thing to them. Together. Mum will believe us!'

If only that were true.

I wondered for a moment how Gabbi would react to finding out that she possibly had another brother out there. Ryan Spencer.

'Gab,' I said gently, 'things are too complicated. I can't go home. The cops don't believe me. Even Mum . . .' I paused. 'Hey,' I said, 'please don't cry on me. One day—soon—I'll be home with you. We'll all be together again. But I have to stay away for now. I have a lot of work to do that I can't do unless I'm out here. In hiding. This secret that I'm working on affects our family. It involves things that belong to us, no-one else. Don't you worry about me, OK? Now let's get you home safely.'

'But what will I tell them about the attack?'

'Just tell them the truth—that you don't remember anything up until tonight. That you were in your room when someone hit you. Just don't mention seeing me here.'

'That's right, Gabs,' said Boges, nodding vigorously. 'And please leave me right out of the picture, too. Otherwise I will be in deep, deep . . . chocolate. I'll come and visit you when you're back home, but we'll have to pretend it's the first time we've seen each other since January, OK?'

'I won't say anything. I promise. I'll just say I woke up in the river, got washed ashore and a

. . . a bushwalker found me. I won't tell them any more than that.'

Gabbi and Boges high-fived each other.

7:00 am

'Off you go, now, Gab,' I said, after releasing her from a tight hug in the back of Sharkey's car. Sharkey had driven us all to a secluded spot a safe distance from the police station. 'I'll see you again soon, I promise.'

Gabbi took Winter's hand and they both slid out of the car. Winter softly closed the door behind them, and silently mouthed, 'Won't be long.' Gab reluctantly looked back at Boges and me through the car window with her bravest face on. We both waved as the pair walked away from us.

They were only a few metres away when Gab dropped Winter's hand and came running back to me, Winter following closely behind.

'How come I'm wearing this?' she said, holding up her hands to me. 'I thought I gave it to you!' She pointed to the little Celtic ring on her finger. 'I did, didn't I? I remember! It was after you nearly drowned in the bay. Back in the holiday house?'

'You did,' I agreed. 'You did give it to me, but then I visited you once—in the hospital—and I put it back on your finger to show you I'd been there.'

'Even though everyone was after you?'

'I snuck in. And I'll visit you again, I promise.'

'But it will be too dangerous!' she protested.

'I'll find a safe way. OK? Now quickly, you'd better get going.'

'Come on, Gabbi,' Winter said, taking my sister's hand again.

But Gabbi stood firm and twisted the Celtic ring right off her finger.

'You have to take this back,' she said, 'It's kept me safe so far. You need it more than me now.'

She passed the silver ring through the window, and I slipped it back onto my pinkie-finger. I looked down at the two interconnecting strands that reminded me of the symbol for eternity.

'When I come home for good, I'll give it back. See you soon, Gab,' I whispered, turning the ring on my finger.

I watched again as the pair walked away. I still couldn't believe Gab was OK, and that Winter—this girl I'd doubted, countless times, risked her own life by jumping into Spindrift River to save mine.

8:54 am

We'd been back on the road for an hour and a half after collecting Winter. Sharkey decided it was safe enough for us to pull over for a quick bathroom break near a picnic spot in the bush.

'Be back here in under ten,' he called out, as the three of us—Winter, Boges and I—wandered off through the bush in different directions.

In the distance, I spotted a family with little kids playing under shady paperbark trees beside the curving lagoon. The trees along the banks reminded me of how Dad used to make toy boats for us when Gab and I were little, playing around the ponds at Richmond Park. He'd use some of the long strips of papery bark that hung down from the massive trees to craft a little hull, then fasten some wafer-thin paperbark on a pointy willow stick to make a sail.

I thought about Gabbi and imagined how shocked the cops back at the station would have been to find her at their door. And, far more exciting than that, I imagined Mum's joy on receiving the news that not only was her daughter found alive, she was out of the coma.

It was almost unbelievable.

I'd lost the Riddle and the Jewel, but Gabbi was safe and well.

It was September. I had less than four months left to sort out the Ormond Singularity before it expired. Or, as the crazy guy warned me, before *I* expired. By December 31st, I told myself, I must find the Riddle and the Jewel, get them back and then somehow get myself over to Ireland . . . All while escaping the clutches of the law, Vulkan Sligo and Oriana de la Force. It seemed impossible, but I was starting to feel convinced that going to Ireland was my only hope of tracking down the missing pieces.

I stared sightlessly ahead as the hugeness of the job in front of me loomed in my mind.

From one of the nearby trees, a magpie warbled.

What should I do next?

The magpie warbled louder. I turned my head, shielding my eyes from harsh sunlight that streamed through a gap in the leaves of the tree I was under.

Within seconds, I was forced to duck as a fast-moving, black and white dive-bomber narrowly missed my face. Sunlight must have reflected from the silver Celtic ring on my finger.

The black and white flurry whooshed past me, then settled on a willow branch growing from a half-submerged tree in the lagoon.

Could it be?

It couldn't. Not a chance.

I squinted.

'Maggers, is that you?' I asked, examining him.

He squawked and ruffled his feathers.

I was sure it was him! He was getting ready for another dive.

'Maggers! It's me! Enough with the dive-bombing, OK?'

At the sound of my voice, Maggers stopped his attack and flew to a lower branch to check me out. I took a step backwards. I wanted to keep my eyeballs in their sockets.

I noticed distinctive black flecks around his white collar, and the small white patch over his right eye. I was almost one hundred per cent sure it was Maggers—Great-uncle Bartholomew's attack bird.

'You're a long way from home, Maggers. What is it?'

'Argle bargle,' he said.

'And the same to you.'

He gave himself a little shake, then flew to the ground, not far from where I was, scratching around contentedly and checking things out with his beak, taking his surroundings in with his intelligent eyes.

It was so good to see him again. As I watched him, I thought of the bug he'd swallowed, and how he'd taken Oriana de la Force's thugs on a wild magpie chase through the bush after Bartholomew figured out they'd been tracking me.

An idea started forming in my mind. An idea

that I hoped would give us the information we so desperately needed—the whereabouts of the Riddle and the Jewel.

'Time to get going,' I said to the magpie. 'See you again some time.'

'Argle bargle,' he said.

9:10 am

I ran back to the car and Maggers stayed close by, flying from tree to tree. I swear that bird was following me.

'I'm sorry, I'm sorry,' I said to Sharkey, Winter and Boges, who were all waiting for me inside the car. 'You won't believe it,' I said as I climbed in the back. 'I saw Maggers!'

'Maggers?' Winter repeated, confused.

'Not the attack bird?' Boges asked, with a dubious chuckle. 'Your great-uncle's magpie?'

'It was him, I swear!'

Sharkey sighed and started the car.

'Look, there he is!' I said, pointing out the window to Maggers, flying above the car.

'You think that bird is Maggers?' said Boges, while exchanging disbelieving looks with Winter. 'As if!'

I ignored him. I sat back and pulled the seatbelt across my chest and clicked it into place. I silently stared out of the window, carefully watching the black and white bird as we began pulling away from the kerb. Eventually, Maggers disappeared into the trees lining the side of the road.

4 SEPTEMBER

119 days to go . . .

5 Enid Parade, Crystal Beach

6:00 pm

Boges had given me the all-clear to stay in the beachside mansion again, until further notice, so I was enjoying it while it lasted. I couldn't believe there were people in the world who were so rich that they could have a house as amazing as this one without even needing to live in it.

Winter and Boges had both had one too many mysterious absences recently to explain to one person or another, so they decided to lie low for a little while to subdue any suspicions. That meant, for now, my life was back to just me, myself and I.

Knowing Gabbi was recovering at her new home—Rafe's place—alive, awake and well, was a massive weight off my shoulders. I almost felt like I could relax a bit. At least until Boges and Winter could get back on the DMO case with me.

I'd been working on my plan to get information from Oriana's, but I needed to wait until Boges was free to see whether he thought we could pull it off.

I didn't want to waste the down time, so I headed for the home theatre room—to get back to working my way through the mansion's extensive movie collection . . .

8 SEPTEMBER

115 days to go . . .

11:20 pm

📱 boges, any chance we can meet up soon? i'm halfway thru the movie collection, but going a bit stir-crazy now . . .

📱 cabin fever, hey? i don't blame u. i have heaps of work 2 do, but me and winter r both free on the 12th. meet u @ hers?

📱 sure. what time?

📱 after 4pm?

📱 perfect. do u remember that air rifle u had years ago? the one u adjusted so we could fire those little plastic parachute soldiers out of it?

📱 sure do. it's here somewhere, buried underneath all my stuff. what about it? where is this leading?

📱 i'll explain @ winter's. can u pls bring it?

📱 ok . . . i'll start digging around for it now. ur not planning a shooting rampage, r u?

📱 nothing like that. there's something else i need too.

📱 let me guess . . . bullets?

📱 haha. no bullets. i need the smallest listening device u can get ur hands on.

9 SEPTEMBER

114 days to go . . .

Outside Oriana de la Force's house

8:54 pm

I was on the street in hiding, scoping out Oriana's house once again, looking for the best vantage point from where I could put my plan into action.

She had improved the security around her house considerably since the last time I'd been snooping, searching for signs of Gabbi. There were small cameras that hadn't been there before. The driveway had a new tall metal gate across it with a serious electronic lock. Another security door had been added to the front entrance.

I considered and rejected a number of possibilities and then I noticed the regrowth on the pine tree from where I'd taken the photo that had revealed the Ormond Riddle. Each lopped-off bough was sprouting fresh green needles, making for more cover than I'd had on my earlier climb.

I'd be safest at night, although that would bring about its own problems. For what I intended to do, I needed some visibility.

12 SEPTEMBER

111 days to go . . .

12 Lesley Street

4:04 pm

I ducked around the back of the apartment block, hauling myself up the fire-escape stairs until I reached the very top. I was starving—I hadn't eaten all day—and was feeling a bit light-headed.

As soon as I stepped onto the roof and looked towards the door of Winter's little flat, I could smell something delicious in the air. My stomach grumbled loudly.

Winter must have just washed her hair because it was all wrapped up on top of her head in a white towel. She was wearing a grey-and-white striped sweater and dark blue jeans. Her face was scrubbed clean. I thought she looked cute and wanted to tell her so, but instead I walked inside and said, 'Something smells good.'

'I made us some lasagne.'

'I love lasagne.'

'Well, you'd better try it before you get too excited. I've never made it before.'

'I'm so hungry right now I could eat almost anything. Although,' I added, 'I'm sure if *you* made it, it will taste delicious.'

'Take a seat,' she said, sliding out a chair for me. 'Like my new desk?' she asked, flashing her eyes over to a neat white table, with ornate, carved legs, that sat in the place of her old one. 'Vulkan didn't even end up bringing it over for me—he sent some other guy around with it.'

'Who did he send?' I asked, wondering who Sligo was counting on to do his dirty work these days. 'Wasn't Red Singlet, was it?'

'Nah, it was Max. You know, the rev-head guy I had to distract when you and Repro broke into the safe? Bruno's been behind bars ever since the shootout in Redcliffe—there was no escaping the cops when he was perched up the bell tower. So Vulkan's been relying on Max a lot more lately.'

'Hell-o?' came Boges's sing-song voice from the front door.

Winter scurried over to let him in, pulling the towel out of her hair in the process. Her hair was longer than I'd ever seen it before. It twisted almost all the way down to her waist.

'Hi!' she said as she greeted Boges.

'What's cookin', good lookin'?' he joked, reaching in for a hug.

'Lasagne,' I called out. 'Sit down, I'm starving.'

Boges came over and squeezed my shoulders before sitting down opposite me. He placed a long duffel bag on the floor, and I hoped it had the air rifle inside it. 'Wow, it smells good,' he said.

'I hope it tastes as good!' said Winter, heaving the dish out of the oven, with the help of red and white, polka-dot oven mitts.

'Dude,' Boges said, ploughing a fork into the giant slice of steaming lasagne that had just landed on his plate. 'I have some information I need to pass on to you. Winter,' he said with his mouth full, 'this is amazing!'

Winter beamed.

'Sure is,' I added, before looking back at Boges, waiting to hear his news.

'I called into Rafe's house and talked to Gabbi yesterday,' he said. 'She looks and sounds so much better; she's getting stronger every day . . . It's so good to have Gabbi back to her old self.'

'That's great to hear, but why are you saying it like it's bad news?' I asked, not liking the tone of his voice.

Boges scratched at his head. It was such a normal thing for him to do, but it looked so different without all of his dark hair flopping about over his hands.

'The media has gone crazy over the story—it's been an absolute frenzy,' he said. 'The paparazzi's camped out the front of Rafe's place 24–7 at the moment. I spoke to your mum, too. She's happy to have Gabbi back but—but—'

'But what?' I asked.

'What?' I repeated, puzzled.

'Look man, don't take this the wrong way. But it's your mum . . .'

'What about her?'

'Gabbi's noticed it too. She thinks she's . . . *changed*. I know we've talked about it before but—I don't know how to put this—she's—' Boges shrugged, gesturing with his open hands. 'Do you think she's taking something? Something to help with all her anxiety and stress?'

'Possibly,' I said. 'I know she's changed. She hasn't been herself since this whole mess began unfolding. It's just all the bad things that have happened to her, building up, overwhelming her.'

Boges shook his head. 'Just as many bad things have happened to you. And to Gabbi. And both of you are still the same person. Gab looks a little different, but every day, as she recovers, she's showing that she's still the same old Gabbi. You've had to toughen up, I know that, but you're still the same Cal Ormond underneath. With your mum, it's something else. I've known her almost all my life, like since I was five. I know how she handles things.'

His face brightened all of a sudden. 'Remember that time when I stacked it off your new red BMX bike, when we were about seven or something? I had blood gushing out of my forehead, and my mum and gran were wailing, completely freaking out about it, running around like headless chooks. But your mum was the one who came over to my side, held my hand and said, all steady and calm, "Well, you've had yourself a bit of an accident, haven't you? Let's get you into the car and go get you patched up." She kept me calm by acting as though all I needed was a bandaid, but I ended up with nine stitches! Look,' Boges said, pointing to a scar high on his forehead that used to be covered up with his long hair. 'Check out that scar!'

'Yikes,' said Winter, leaning across the table to have a closer look. 'I've never noticed it before.'

'Cal's mum was always the calming voice of reason,' he explained to Winter. 'Even when his dad died, she was the rock. Wasn't she?' he said to me.

'She was the rock in tough situations,' I agreed.

Sadness gripped my heart. That part of Mum's personality felt like a distant memory.

Boges paused and took a deep breath, and the concern on his face brought me back to reality.

'I'm going to talk really straight, dude. I think she's taking way too many pills, or something. It's like she's in la-la land. I mean, there's no way she would be acting like this—this weird, detached woman who almost switched her own daughter's life support off, and who believes her son is a murderer. Not the Mrs Ormond I've known all my life.' Boges fiddled with his fork. 'No offence.'

'No offence taken.' I thought some more before I spoke again. 'You know, the few times I've spoken to Mum, since all this happened, I have felt like she wasn't really there. It's weird because even when Dad was dying, and even after he died, Mum didn't take anything for the pain. He was her best friend, her soul mate, her life . . . and he was taken away. But she fought through it with nothing but sheer will.'

Winter put her hand on mine.

'What has Gabbi said about it?' I asked.

Boges shook his head. 'Nothing about medication. But she said she's really worried. She had a bit of a tear in her eye when I saw her. She asked me if I thought there was something wrong with your mum. Rafe's really worried, too. You can see it in the way he looks at her. Maybe it's not pills. Maybe she's . . .' His voice trailed off but I knew what he was thinking.

'You're thinking she might be having a breakdown? Going crazy or something with all the stress?'

'I don't know, Cal. At least now she has Gabbi back safely. That might help calm her down a bit.'

'Is Gabbi going to be safe there?' I asked. 'She was kidnapped from there once before. Have they upped the security?'

'She'll be fine at Rafe's place. The security there is tight as,' Boges said. 'Rafe's had all sorts of new gadgets, bars and alarms installed for protection. He walked me around the perimeter, explaining everything to me. Pretty impressive. He's done his research. He knows what he's talking about.'

Thank goodness, I thought. Although it would make it very hard for me to visit Gabbi.

'It's weird how much he looks like your dad,' said Boges. 'I mean, I know they're identical twins, but I never really saw the similarities in them before.' Suddenly distracted, he eyed a chocolate cake that Winter had begun unveiling, from underneath a tea towel. 'No way, you made chocolate cake for me too?'

Winter's flat was starting to look like the operations room in a TV police show. We had our notes spread everywhere. The photos from Ireland and Dad's drawings were stuck against cupboards or propped up on the counter so that wherever you looked there was something to study, something to consider. The freaky little monkey puzzled me a lot. He didn't seem to fit in anywhere at all. What could he possibly mean?

'So it was Oriana de la Force behind the kidnapping,' said Boges, munching through a second slice of cake. 'We think she has the Ormond Riddle and the Ormond Jewel. And now she has the drawings too—*thinks* she has the drawings—' he corrected, throwing an admiring look at Winter.

'Yes,' I said. 'Now she thinks she has everything. Which is good in a way, because it gets her off our back. I hope. And now that Gabbi's safe, the next thing to do is—'

'Get the Riddle and the Jewel back,' Winter finished for me. 'It's not going to be easy. From what you said about her place, it'll be like Rafe's place—trying to get past security at Fort Knox.'

We sat in silence for a few moments; the only sound in the flat was the distant traffic rising up from below. I realised my mind was always scanning background noises. Anything resembling a siren made me edgy.

'But check this,' Boges said, pulling out a folded printed page from his pocket.

'What is it?' I asked, leaning over to take it from him.

'I found this on your blog last night.'

Inbox

To: C. Ormond

From: T. Brinsley

Dear Mr Callum Ormond,

I work as the manuscript keeper at Trinity College, Dublin, in a position called 'Keeper of Rare Books'. Your story has become quite famous—for all the wrong reasons—but coming from my position, I know a little more than most about your predicament and have no difficulty in believing in your innocence. I understand how powerful the lure of the Ormond Singularity is, and how it has tempted criminal interests. You have most unfortunately been caught up in its complicated web.

I want you to know that I have some information to pass on about the Ormond Riddle. I am sure you're aware, at this stage, that there are two missing lines. It would be ideal if you could bring the original manuscript of the Riddle to Ireland, but I know this may prove beyond your powers, given your current circumstances.

If you are able to make the trip, please do get in touch. I have always had an interest in the Ormond family and its secrets. My mother was a Butler from Carrick-on-Suir.

Sincerely,

Dr Theophilus Brinsley

The missing two lines! Could it be true?

'I guess we can look into this guy,' I said. 'I mean, make sure he is who he says he is. That he really works at Trinity College; that he really is the Keeper of Rare Books. If he checks out,' I said, my excitement building, 'this could be awesome! I wonder if Dad met this guy when he was in Ireland.'

'You should call Eric Blair again,' said Boges. 'He was willing to talk, right? He might know about him. We have to be careful—who knows if we can trust this *Dr Theophilus Brinsley*—but if he's legit, we could already have an ally over there who has crucial information for us about the Ormond Singularity.'

'We have to go to Ireland,' Winter announced matter-of-factly.

Boges looked at her, a little surprised. 'That won't be easy.'

'Now that's an understatement,' she replied. 'But I'm serious. We have to. Ireland is where it all started. We have to get the Riddle and the Jewel back, and we have to go to Ireland.'

'Yep,' I agreed. 'It's where Dad first stumbled on the amazing secret to do with our family. And it's where his investigations ended—where he got sick, where he had to leave it behind before coming back home to the hospice.'

'It's where the photos come from,' added Winter. 'We still have those, don't we?'

'Over there,' I said, pointing to them. 'I didn't hand them over.'

'Great. We need to check all of those locations out.'

I nodded. 'We don't have any choice. It's really our last hope. Winter's right. We have to go to Ireland.'

'Look, talking about this is all well and good, but how do you think we're going to get there? Do I need to remind you that you're a wanted criminal? I don't have a passport. Neither do you. And even if you did have one, you'd be tracked down and arrested in seconds. You'd be on a watch list at every airport out of the country. Plus we're going to need a few thousand bucks.'

Boges was right. 'I know all that,' I conceded. 'We can't do it right now. But that doesn't mean we can't work towards it. Maybe Sharkey can help us out.'

'More than ever, we have to find the Riddle and the Jewel,' said Boges.

'I told you I have a plan,' I said, 'that I hope will help make that happen.'

'Something to do with this?' he said, reaching for a pocket in his duffel bag. He lifted out a small object in a blister pack and placed it on the table in front of us.

'I could only afford one. It's the latest from Russia—made under magnification—using nano-technology,' Boges explained. 'The latest in nanotechnology at least for the Russians. The Israelis and Americans probably have better gear, but it's not available to people like me yet. This pretty much cleaned out my savings, dude.'

'Unreal,' I said, barely hearing him as I picked up the packet, examining the small, round object inside. 'Thanks. This reminds me of the bug that Oriana de la Force implanted in my shoulder,' I added, picking up the tiny device with my thumb and forefinger.

'Cal, what's going on? I can't stand the sus-pense,' said Winter, twisting her wild hair up into a knot on the top of her head. I smiled, thinking of how she used to torment me in the same way, teasing me by taking her time telling me something I was dying to know.

'It's a tiny transmitter, tuned to a particular radio frequency,' Boges explained, 'but the band-width is way under the usual station numbers you have on a regular radio. This transmits at around 32–33 megahertz. All we need then is an FM receiver tuned to pick up that wavelength.

Then we can pick up whatever this little sucker broadcasts.'

'And then we can listen in?' Winter asked. 'Just like listening to the radio?'

'That's right,' said Boges, 'except for just one little problem. We can only listen for a limited amount of time.'

'How limited?'

'Probably not more than ten to twelve hours.'

'I don't get it,' I said. 'Oriana was on my tail for months, not hours.'

'This thing's different. It's a listening device with a little microphone. The bug implanted in your shoulder only sent out a tiny signal. It didn't use much power. Like your watch battery. This one needs much more energy to work.'

'So you're going to bug Oriana?' Winter asked.

Boges and I nodded slowly.

'If we can listen in to her conversations,' I said, 'I feel sure we'll hear something. Something that will give us an idea of where she's hidden the Riddle and the Jewel.'

'We're not going to hear very much unless we're close,' explained Boges. 'We probably need to be within five hundred metres of wherever you put the transmitter.'

'But how are you going to get the bug inside Oriana's house?' Winter asked.

'It was Maggers who gave me the idea,' I said. 'I saw him again, remember?'

'So you're going to fly through a window like a bird?' Winter asked, in her old mocking tone.

'Something like that,' I replied, looking over at Boges, hoping he'd brought the air rifle in his duffel bag.

Right on cue, he unzipped it and lifted the projectile weapon out of its casing.

'You're going to shoot the bug into Oriana de la Force's house!' cried Winter.

'Do you think you can do it?' I asked Boges. 'Attach the bug to something that can be fired?'

'I know I can do it,' said Boges, confidently. 'No problem. I still have heaps of those darts we used to fire from the air rifle when we ran out of our little parachute soldiers.'

'They mostly ended up stuck in trees,' I explained to Winter. 'Or on rooftops.'

'You'll only get one chance at it,' she said. 'Better make it a good shot.'

The three of us looked at each other in silence.

'It's a good plan, dude. I couldn't have thought of a better way in myself. I'll get to work on creating a carrier for the bug, contributing some of my brilliant brainpower.'

'Sure you have any left?' Winter asked. 'Now

that you've lost your curls? Remember Samson? He lost all his strength when his hair was cut.'

'When he was betrayed by that evil chick, Delilah,' Boges reminded her.

'I'm sure she had her reasons,' Winter came back fast at him.

'You know the big pine tree that I climbed up way back?' I cut into their banter. 'When I took that photo of Oriana? I'm going to use that tree again—climb up until I'm opposite the window, take aim and with a bit of luck I'll fire the bug right in. By then, Boges, you will have adapted it for me, so that it sticks to the wall across from the window. Somewhere it won't be noticed.'

'Leave it to me, dude. I'll design something that no-one will take any notice of—even if they see it.'

'Cool,' I said. 'Like what?'

'I'll surprise you.'

'Boges, speaking of surprises . . . What did you tell your mum,' asked Winter, 'about your new hairstyle?'

Boges ran a hand over his now finely bristled dome.

'I kind of made something up,' he said, sheepishly. 'I said I did it for charity.'

'For charity? You lied about charity?'

'I know, I didn't know what to say! But what

better charity case than helping to save Gabbi? I can't think of one.'

I couldn't either, when he put it like that.

'Gran just about fainted when she saw it. Thought there was an intruder in the house. Mum had to calm her down.'

'I kind of like it,' said Winter.

Boges threw me a look. 'Maddy likes it, too.'

Winter raised an eyebrow.

I turned my attention back to business, pulling out my mobile. 'I'm going to email Dr Brinsley.'

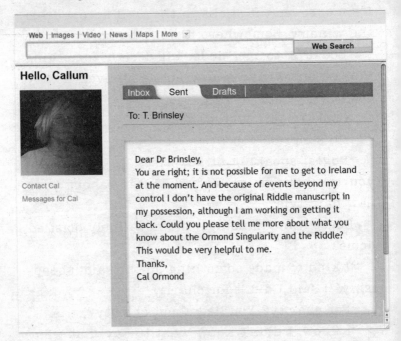

Web | Images | Video | News | Maps | More

Web Search

Hello, Callum

Contact Cal
Messages for Cal

Inbox   Sent   Drafts

To: T. Brinsley

Dear Dr Brinsley,
You are right; it is not possible for me to get to Ireland at the moment. And because of events beyond my control I don't have the original Riddle manuscript in my possession, although I am working on getting it back. Could you please tell me more about what you know about the Ormond Singularity and the Riddle? This would be very helpful to me.
Thanks,
Cal Ormond

15 SEPTEMBER

108 days to go . . .

S Enid Parade, Crystal Beach

2:10 pm

I couldn't do anything much about bugging Oriana de la Force's place until Boges had modified the listening device and the air rifle chamber. But I had made another trip to her house to monitor the premises. Keeping well back, I watched the comings and goings, trying to get a sense of the rhythm of Oriana's days and the movements of the bodyguards who were looking out for her. They patrolled at regular intervals, at more or less the same time every day and night.

Back in the mansion, I decided to call Eric Blair.

'Eric Blair,' he said. With just two words, I could tell he was much more confident and together than the last time I spoke to him.

'Mr Blair, it's Cal.'

There was a stunned silence which I rushed to fill before he could say anything. 'Last time

I called you said you'd be happy to talk to me. Can you talk now?'

'Is that really you, Cal? I didn't think you'd call me again. Not after you gave me a dud number last time.'

'Sorry about that. My phone was out of action. Please believe me when I say that I had nothing to do with the crimes that I've been charged with. I haven't hurt anyone. I've been caught up in a . . . in a mess that's been out of my control. I'm desperately trying to clear my name and track down something concerning my family and our future. I'm really hoping you can help me.'

'Cal,' he said, 'I know you're innocent.'

'You do?'

Was he for real or was this a trick? Had he warned the police that I said I was going to call him again?

'I do,' was all he said in reply.

'I'm hoping you can help me out with information about Dad and those days you spent together in Ireland—'

'OK,' he said, cutting me short. 'I'm more than happy to pass on whatever I can, but I can't do it right now—I'm just about to fly out to cover the climate change conference in Lisbon. I'll call you when I'm back again and we'll work something out. Very carefully, of course.'

'Sure, I understand.' Aiding and abetting a wanted criminal would not look good on Mr Blair's resume.

'Are you safe?' he asked.

'I'm safe,' I said, surprised by his concern. 'I'm getting pretty good at flying beneath the radar.'

'Good, well give me your number and I will call you as soon as I'm back in the country.'

17 SEPTEMBER

106 days to go . . .

12 Lesley Street

8:15 pm

When Winter finally opened her door, it was obvious she'd been crying.

'Hey,' I said, dumping my backpack on the floor. 'What's wrong? What is it?'

'Oh, nothing, just the usual stuff,' she said, going into the little bathroom and looking at her reflection in the mirror. 'I can never get away with crying without everyone who sees me knowing about it. My eyes always go so red and puffy.' She splashed water on her face, and then dried herself on the hand towel nearby. She stood in the doorway with her hands on her hips, looking defeated—something I rarely saw in her. 'Sometimes,' she said with a sigh, 'I think I'll never find out what really happened to them.'

'To your parents?'

She nodded. 'I know there's no use crying about it. Crying's not going to find me any answers.'

We both wandered over to the couch and let ourselves fall into it.

'Cal, will you help me with something?'

'Of course I will. What is it?'

'I need you to help me find the car.'

9:21 pm

Winter and I hurried through the night, heads down against the cold wind that was blowing from the north-west.

She was wearing the same dark brown hoodie, pulled up around her face, that she was wearing that night back in February, when I'd seen her prowling around the car yard and mistaken her for a boy. All of her hair was tucked away, out of sight, and she was wearing jeans and boots. Clearly she didn't want anyone recognising her.

'Any news on Sligo getting you your own car?' I asked, as we both rushed along on foot.

She laughed. 'No, Max says he's working on it, but I don't think it will happen any time soon. Your legs will just have to put up with it for now.'

I groaned, loudly.

'Are you sure you want to do this with me?' she asked.

'Of course I am. You've helped me out so much.

Not to mention saving my life. But that's not the reason,' I said. 'We're friends. That's what friends do, right?'

Winter Frey really has the best smile, I thought to myself.

Car yard

10:11 pm

I shivered, remembering the first time I'd been here, the brutal interrogation and the terror of the fast-filling oil tank.

'This place gives me the creeps,' I said as we hurried down the road past the high wire fence that surrounded the yard, heading around the corner where the main gates were. 'I'm not sure I understand what we're doing here exactly.'

Winter paused and pulled me under the shelter of an overhanging peppercorn tree.

'I'm trying to find the car—my parents' car.'

I frowned. 'But haven't you already searched this place?'

'When I was here the other day, I noticed that a section of the yard—a row of cars—had been shifted, which means I can now access the pile of wrecks that were behind them.'

'OK, but the car was involved in a fatal accident; wouldn't it have gone to a police car yard?'

'Yes, until the *accident* investigation was finished.'

'What do you mean—*accident*?' I asked. 'Are you saying you think there was foul play involved?'

Winter shrugged off my question.

'Wouldn't it have been destroyed?' I continued.

'Look, Cal, I have to find out for sure. If it's not here, it's not here. But I just have this feeling something *is* here, waiting for me to find it. It doesn't make sense, but something keeps drawing me back. Cars are usually destroyed,' she said, 'but in this case, things were different. Sligo was friends with one of the local cops at Boronia Ridge—near where the crash happened— and that cop did the original investigation. I saw the report about a year after it happened. Sligo's signature was scrawled across the receipt, which means the car went to his yard.'

Winter paused to tuck a strand of loose hair back up into her hoodie.

'The investigation found that Dad had lost control of the car on that sharp bend,' she continued. 'They said speed was involved and that wet weather and worn brakes played their part, too. But, I swear, Dad was so protective of me and Mum . . . he would never have put us both in danger by speeding. And I remember . . . I think I remember . . . he was shocked when it happened. Something was wrong. The car skidded out of control and slammed off the road. I was thrown out, unharmed, while Mum and Dad crashed down the side of the mountain.'

She turned away to hide the tears in her eyes. I took her hand.

'I just need to see the car,' she sobbed. 'I just need to see it.'

'It's OK,' I said. 'You need to see the car, so let's go find it.'

10:23 pm

Winter selected a key from her key ring and quickly unlocked the padlock that connected the gates.

'You have a key to Sligo's car yard?' I asked.

'I have the keys to a lot of things.'

We slipped through quickly and Winter connected the two gates together again loosely, without locking it. That suited me. A quick getaway should always be factored in.

'Here,' she said, handing me a small black torch from her bag. She pulled out an identical one for herself.

'Where are we going to start?' I wondered, looking at the sprawling jumble of old car bodies. Some were half hidden under rotting tarpaulins, some were piled on top of each other like stacks of squashed beetles. The rusty chrome and paint-work reflected our torchlight as we moved.

'We need to be careful not to activate the sensor lights. Let's stay as far from the building as possible,' she said, as we headed off down a walkway between the car bodies. Winter waved her left arm, indicating the crowded tangle of cars on the side closest to the road we'd come along. 'It's not as bad as it looks. I've done all of this side, and I've been through that entire area up there behind the office.' She pointed to an area on our far right. 'That's where I want to go. That's the lot that couldn't be accessed before.'

'Hey,' I said, 'let's just make sure there's no-one in the office.' I'd learned to be very cautious in my months on the run. I didn't take anything for granted.

The office block appeared to be in darkness.

'There's no-one there,' she said. I hoped she knew what she was talking about. 'Don't go any closer,' she warned, again. 'You don't want to set off the sensor lights.'

'No,' I agreed. 'Let's keep the noise down and stay down low.'

'That's the plan,' she said with a smirk that was barely visible in the darkness.

'So what are we looking for?' I asked.

'A gold 2002 BMW,' she said, 'with cream and tan upholstery. And with a little something extra on the upholstery in the back.'

'Something extra?'

I saw a series of expressions move across her face—love, sadness, anger and determination.

'I'll show you if . . . *when* we find it.'

I slipped an arm around her. 'Let's go,' I said. 'You start here, and I'll go up the rise and start working down towards you,' I pointed to the further pile of cars on higher ground.

'Deal. We'll meet up somewhere in the middle.'

I wandered away, trailing behind the light of my torch.

10:44 pm

It wasn't a difficult search, but there were a heck of a lot of cars. Many of them were still in pretty good condition and their paintwork was clearly visible by torchlight. Others had been crushed and compacted into rectangular shapes—their colours and makes were more difficult to identify. I didn't waste time on any vehicles except the gold ones.

Sometimes, I had to get down on my hands and knees to check cars on the bottom of the piles. All sorts of vehicles were there: family sedans crushed and rusting, utes with murky water collected in the corners of their trays, truck cabins and the occasional trailer, all squashed together without any sort of order.

At one point as I worked my way through, moving my torchlight ahead of me, I found a mother cat with three kittens on the back seat of a very old Ford. I was about to call out to Winter—I thought she'd like to see the kittens—when she called out to me herself.

'I found it! Cal! It's here! It's here! Mum and Dad's car!'

I jumped down from where I was and as I landed an automatic light came on nearby, flooding the area. Now I could clearly see Winter on her hands and knees, peering into the wreck of a car, completely oblivious to the fact that the light had just come on.

'Over here, Cal! Quick! I found it!'

I ran over to her. She'd jumped up now and was anxiously shining her torch through other car bodies and peering through them. 'It's not going to be easy to get to. We'll have to somehow crawl through those old cars in front to get to it.'

'How do you know it's the one? It has no plates, nothing. It could be anyone's car.'

'I just do!' she said, stopping to look up at me. Her face was shining with joy and hope.

'OK, let's find a way in.'

I was just about to duck down to join her, when I saw a huge shadow separate itself from the darkness behind the office building.

The sensor light, and probably Winter's shrieks, had alerted unwanted company.

'There's someone coming!' I said, reaching for her boots to pull her out. 'Get up!'

'But the car, it's right here!'

The huge shadow was racing up behind us, growing with every second.

I grabbed both of Winter's boots and pulled her out of the wreck. 'We have to run!'

As we both got to our feet another automatic light switched on.

My jaw dropped.

It couldn't be!

It was impossible!

I'd seen him fall out of the bell tower and into the sky! I'd seen him lying dead in the splintered cactus plants out the front of the convent! Zombrovski had broken his neck when he messed up his attempt to kill me!

'Zombie Two,' I heard Winter whisper. 'Run!'

Winter was closer to Zombie Two and he was about to pounce on her. He lunged, knocking the torch out of her hand. It skidded with great speed out to the side.

Zombie Two's massive hands went for Winter's throat, and I instinctively hurtled myself at him, jumping onto his back and trying hopelessly to drag him away from her.

He flung me off his back like he was flicking a bug.

I tumbled to the ground.

Zombie Two released his grip on Winter and came after me.

He loomed over me as I scuttled backwards. He picked up the wayward torch and shone it right in my face.

His face began contorting with fury as recognition registered in his mind.

'It's you!' he hissed in a thick, foreign accent. Winter was right: Zombie Two was even bigger and uglier than his brother! I never imagined it could be true. His eyes bulged, as if his anger was making them explode out of his head. He leaned back, nostrils flaring. 'You kill my brother!'

'But I—'

'You kill my brother!'

'But I didn't! He—'

'You,' he shouted, like he was possessed, 'kill my brother!'

Zombie Two was going to kill me, no question. He grabbed my throat. He was crushing the air out of me. I could smell his stinking breath as he glowered over me, roaring. His hands were tightening remorselessly around my throat, and he was pinning me to the ground with his huge bulk.

Out of the corner of my eye, I thought I could see Winter coming up behind him.

'You kill my brother—now I kill you!' he screeched. 'You break his neck—I break yours!'

But before he knew it, something struck Zombie Two on his back!

He roared in pain and fell forward. His hands dropped from my throat.

Winter stood behind him, awkwardly clutching a massive steel bumper bar! She looked as shocked as I was. I rolled away from Zombie Two and climbed to my feet.

'Run!' Winter suddenly screamed, dropping the bumper bar on the ground. It clanged and clattered as we both bolted.

I drew in rasping, pain-filled breaths, clutching my bruised throat as we both ran.

Headlights flashed at the double gates. I heard the sound of voices shouting. I grabbed Winter's arm. 'Come on! Down the other end through the gate in the fence!'

She didn't have to be told twice. We both took off, ducking and weaving through the piles of cars, racing towards the back gate in the fence through which we'd escaped on the very first night we'd met.

Behind us, the sounds of Zombie Two's groans and curses faded as we pelted away.

18 SEPTEMBER

105 days to go . . .

12 Lesley Street

12:02 am

'We have to go back, Cal,' Winter said between puffs. We'd just made it back to her house. 'We have to go back. Now that I know the car is there!'

Wearily, I straightened up. 'We will,' I said, hoping, for her sake, that it really was the car she'd been searching for. 'But not right now, OK?'

'I'm not crazy!' she said. 'I can't believe I found it! I knew it was there! I just knew it!' Winter gave me a friendly shove on the shoulder.

'Ouch!'

'Oops, sorry. Give us a look,' she said, motioning towards my neck.

I lifted my head up as she examined me by the light of a lamp.

'That's nasty,' she said, prodding my throat. 'Zombie Two got you good.'

'Nearly,' I said. 'How's yours?'

'OK, thanks to you jumping on him. Any longer and I think he would have crushed me.'

'Yeah, it could have turned nasty back there.'

'*Turned* nasty? Any more nasty and you'd be dead, Cal Ormond.'

She was right, although I didn't want to admit it. She'd saved my life in the car yard. Twice.

'Wanna crash here tonight?'

'Sure. Thanks. Do you think Zombie Two realised who you were?' I asked Winter. She'd had her hair tucked away, and most of her face was covered, but we sure didn't want Zombie Two reporting back to Sligo that he'd found her prowling around the car yard. Or, worse, that she was helping out the enemy.

'Don't think so,' she said dismissively. 'Hope not,' she added.

8:15 am

I woke to gentle knocking on the door, and instantly pulled my blanket off me and jumped up from the couch.

'Winter?' came the voice from the door. It was Boges!

I approached the door slowly, just to make sure.

'Winter, it's Boges,' he said.

'Well, hello, Bodhan,' I said, opening the door, in my best Winter impersonation.

Boges jumped back. 'Yikes, I've heard of people not looking their best in the morning,' he joked, 'but wow, Winter, this is extreme!'

'Get in,' I said, pulling my friend through the door and closing it again.

'Boges!' said Winter excitedly from her bed.

'Hi, I was hoping you'd both be here. I have a message to give you from Gabbi,' he said to me.

'Yeah?' I said, excited to hear from my sister. 'What did she say?'

'She said she misses you and that she loves and would you please hurry up and solve the Dangerous Mystery of the Ormonds so that you can come home again?'

I smiled. Winter's mobile started ringing. She snatched it up.

'Yes?'

She nodded a few times, said 'OK,' then hung up. She looked up at both of us, her brows drawn together in a frown. 'Sorry, guys, but you have to get out of here. Right now. That was my tutor. I have fifteen minutes to revise the subjunctive mood in French.'

'The *what*?'

'Never mind. She's on her way. Please, just

go, Cal. You too, Boges. I'm sorry to rush you out, but I have to.'

'OK,' I said, quickly gathering up my things. 'I'll just go back to the beachside mansion.'

I was hauling my backpack over my shoulder when I noticed the look on Boges's face.

'Uh-oh,' I said. 'Don't tell me . . . It's off limits?'

'I'm afraid so,' he said. 'That's what I also wanted to tell you. The owners are finally coming back, so Uncle Sammy and I have a couple of days to clean the place before they show up.' He shrugged. 'Sorry dude, maybe this will help a little.'

He passed me a fifty dollar note. I nodded my thanks to him and pocketed it.

'Out! Out! Out!' said Winter, frantically herding us to the door. 'Please, take it outside. I'll have to catch up with you later!'

8:45 am

'Where will you go?' Boges asked. We were outside on the street and were about to go our separate ways.

I'd had enough of living in drains or trying to sleep in squats and doorways. I knew where there was one safe hideout . . .

'I think I'll try Repro's,' I said.

Repro's Lair

10:09 am

Avoiding eye contact and keeping my head down, I hurried towards the disused railway buildings and slipped through the collapsed fence, heading to the old deserted yard where three large filing cabinets quietly rusted against the rock face behind them.

I hadn't seen Repro since our raid on Sligo's place when we finally laid our hands on the Ormond Jewel. I wasn't sure what sort of reception I'd get from him, but I was keen to find shelter in a safe place, and also to catch up on his news about what had been happening with him since. I sure had plenty to tell him.

I'd grabbed a couple of toasted ham and cheese sandwiches on my way, and hoped that'd help soften him up.

After checking no-one was around, I walked up to the centre filing cabinet and began knocking inside. I opened the paper bags the sandwiches were in, enough to allow the delicious smells to waft through the cracks and into Repro's nostrils.

'Repro,' I called in a low voice. 'It's Cal. Can I come in?'

I heard him grumbling and harrumphing and muttering to himself.

'I've brought us something to eat,' I said. 'How about you let me in and we'll set the table?'

'What do you want?' he finally asked. 'I seem to end up in all sorts of trouble whenever I get mixed up with you.'

'I just want to talk.'

'What about?'

'How about we discuss it over breakfast?'

I could hear more grumbling and muttering behind the wall, and didn't like my chances.

Finally I heard the sound of him releasing the wall.

I pressed against it and it swung open, letting me in. I stood once again looking around at the strange, dim room in which Repro lived among his ever-expanding collection.

He was wearing the same dark green suit with the too-short sleeves that he had been wearing the very first time I'd seen him. His wispy hair had become thinner and today he was wearing a thick pair of rimless glasses that magnified his possum's eyes.

'Ha! You've grown two inches since I saw you last, bailing out of that truck. Two inches!' His eyes shone behind the thick spectacles. 'What a day that was. I hope you're not going to try and involve me in something like that again!'

'No, no,' I said, wondering whether I really

had grown that much. 'What happened to you that day? We pulled up in the truck and then I couldn't see you anywhere. Vanished into thin air?'

'I wish that was something I could do,' he said with a grin. 'That would be an exceptionally handy talent to have.'

'Sure would,' I agreed. There had been endless times I'd wished I could vanish.

'But there's no magic in these bones, I'm afraid,' he said with a disappointed sigh. 'Except for in these safe-cracking fingers!' he said, wriggling them wildly in front of me.

He pulled out a chair for me and cleared the table, shoving a box of key rings with little snowmen on them to the side.

'I ran into the long grass,' Repro explained. 'I called out for you to follow me, but you stopped and went the other way! To the cliff! This kid's done for, I said to myself. Done for! I ducked down, watching, waiting to see what you were going to do . . . and then I saw you take off into the sky!'

'I landed it!' I said, proudly, recalling my flight in the glider. 'Didn't think I was going to, but I made it!'

'Incredible. Incredible,' Repro said, washing his hands in his small sink.

'What's with the thick glasses?' I said, pulling out our sandwiches and placing them on the table. Repro dragged an ancient armchair over, removed the cartons and boxes from it, then sat down.

'It's an image thing,' he replied. 'I read a very informative article in a magazine.' He pointed to a towering pile of magazines and lifted his glasses off before repositioning them, blinking through the lenses. 'I think they give me gravitas,' he said solemnly.

'Gravit-ass?' I repeated. 'Sounds like it might be uncomfortable to sit down.'

'No, no. *Gravitas*,' he repeated slowly. 'Dignity, nobility, grave seriousness, that sort of thing.' He paused for a moment, posing, looking over the tops of the glass. 'The problem is,' he added, slowly sitting down, 'they lend gravitas, but I can't see through them all that well.'

Regardless, his vision seemed to be spot on when it came to the sandwiches. His long, bony fingers whisked one off the table and down his throat with great speed.

'The other problem,' he said, taking a pause from munching on his sandwich, 'is that no-one's ever around to see just how dignified, noble and gravely serious I look!'

11:21 am

All the food was well and truly finished by the time I had filled Repro in on my latest adventures.

He leaned back in the old armchair. 'You mean to tell me after all my hard work with these,' he rubbed and twirled his fingers so fast they blurred, 'that you've gone and lost the Ormond Jewel?'

'I didn't lose it, Repro. Like I told you, I had no option.'

He grunted, nodding, peering at me again over his new glasses. 'So what do you intend to do now?'

'Get them back. Then work out how we can get ourselves to Ireland.'

In turn, Repro told me what he'd been up to. He'd been 'borrowing' more and more objects from the trains before they were collected and locked up by Lost Property.

'You'll never believe what I found packed away in a box!' He jumped up from the armchair in excitement, stepping behind the central bookcases. 'All nicely strung together.'

'Umm,' I said, trying to guess, 'a pearl necklace?'

Suddenly the light went out and I was sitting alone in the darkness.

'Hey!' I yelled. 'What's going on?'

'Boo!' he called out. I nearly jumped out of my skin as Repro danced out from behind his bookcase, switching the light back on to show he was holding up a full skeleton.

'Say g'day to Mr Bones!'

'Repro!' I yelled. 'Are you trying to give me a heart attack?'

'What do you think? He has to be worth a few hundred dollars! Crazy thing is, he's the second skeleton I've found! Mr and Mrs Bones I call them.'

I sank back down on my seat. My heart was pounding. 'You should pay me the few hundred dollars as compensation for taking years off my life!'

I heard his chuckle as he disappeared again, returning Mr Bones to wherever he'd come from.

'The least you can do now,' I said as he plonked down in his crooked armchair, 'is offer me shelter here for a little while . . .'

Repro threw me a sneaky sideways glance. He ignored my suggestion.

At least he hadn't said no.

8:35 pm

The two of us sat around all day and well into the night talking. I told him all about the Zombrovski brothers, the fatal fall of the younger one, and how Zombie Two, even meaner and tougher than his dead brother, was just one more killer enemy I had to look out for.

'There are some mean people around,' said Repro. 'I saw a pair of young terrors just a couple of days ago when I was out getting supplies. They were hanging around, looking like they were up to no good. One guy looked like a pirate with a bandana; the other had a finger missing.'

Three-O and friends? No way!

'I know those guys,' I said, frustrated to be hearing about them. 'They are very bad news. Keep away from them.'

I got up and collapsed into Repro's sagging couch. 'Ah,' I said, stretching my legs out. 'It's so comfortable here.' It was an obvious attempt to convince him to let me stay. I crossed my arms behind my head and yawned loudly.

He picked up an army blanket and threw it at me.

'OK, OK,' he said, with a grin. 'You can stay.'

19 SEPTEMBER

104 days to go . . .

10:30 am

Repro was standing the two skeletons next to each other when I approached him with his cup of tea. He'd popped a floral, straw hat and a string of beads on one, and had draped an army overcoat and an eye patch on the other.

He looked at me for my reaction as he wedged a pipe in the rattling teeth of the skeleton in the overcoat.

'What a good-looking pair, eh?' he joked.

'Sure are,' I said as I passed him his tea. 'Listen, I'm going to try and visit my sister later today.'

'Your sister? Didn't you say your uncle has the place all locked up? You only just got your sister back. You don't want to go and mess it all up by getting caught now.'

'No, I do not want to do that. But I *do* want to see Gabbi. Even if she doesn't see me. I just need to know she's OK. For myself.'

'Right, right. One has to look after his family,' Repro agreed. 'Family is most important. You do whatever you have to do. Just don't let anyone follow you back here.'

Outside Rafe's House
Surfside Street, Dolphin Point

7:35 pm

I'd slipped out from Repro's at dusk. For the outing, I'd borrowed a black jacket, a beanie and a pair of binoculars from his collection.

By the time I reached Rafe's house, it was dark. On the way, I'd picked up a handful of leaflets, advertising a local house painter and gardener, which someone had abandoned near an overflowing bin. I had to be careful not to raise suspicion by hanging around this expensive end of town, so whenever anyone passed me by I pretended I was merely dropping the leaflets into letterboxes.

Cautiously, I peered through the front gate. The street outside was quiet, but I had to make sure I wasn't going to get caught on any cameras or set off any alarms if I came too close to the house. I'd promised Gabbi I'd visit her, even though I knew it wouldn't be easy. I needed to be exceptionally careful.

I pulled out the binoculars to take a better look.

A couple of lights were on upstairs, and one seemed to be switched on near the rear of the house—a terrace area where I recalled Rafe had an outdoor table setting. I scanned the top edges of the house, counting the cameras and sensors that were perched beneath the roof guttering. I worked out the best way in, dodging the scope of the surveillance equipment.

I hoped that the narrow path I had plotted out was going to work for me. If not, I'd be in big trouble.

At the bushiest spot along the fence line, I climbed up and over. I landed almost silently on the other side.

The yard seemed greener and denser than when I'd been here before with Boges, all that time ago in January, looking for the envelope containing my dad's drawings.

I sidled along the fence, trying to work out exactly where Gabbi would be. Not only were there cameras and sensors, but there were grilles on every window. On the entrance foyer were bifold steel mesh doors.

Upstairs, in the middle of the front of the house, there were two windows with a soft light behind them. I felt pretty sure that was where

Gabbi's new room was. I started making my way up a tree, to get a better look in. From my position—facing the house, but just to the side—I could see what was going on out the front, and down one side leading to the backyard.

7:46 pm

Another light came on in the house. It was the room that I recalled had been Rafe's study, where I'd first seen the scribbled phrase, 'Ormond Riddle'. A silhouette, which I guessed was Rafe, moved past the window.

I shuffled into a more stable position in the tree so that I could free my hands to use the binoculars once more.

Through them, everything was much clearer. I could see Gabbi's old furniture—her dressing table and cupboard—in the room I had guessed was hers.

All of a sudden she walked past my vision.

My heart started racing. I wanted to shout out to her. Tell her to come outside.

She was wandering around the room, moving things here and there. She was wearing a pink nightie and white, fluffy slippers.

Rafe's silhouette appeared in her doorway. I watched as Gabbi turned in his direction.

She ran over to him, hugging his waist. He

leaned down and kissed her on the forehead, before leaving the room again.

For a moment it had looked like Dad was in there with her.

8:03 pm

How was I going to let Gabbi know I was there? That I'd come to see her?

Just as I was racking my brain for an idea, Gabbi pulled open one of her bedroom windows. She was leaning on the window sill and staring out, through the bars, into the night sky.

Whenever Dad used to go away on overseas trips, he'd tell both of us to look out into the night sky and stare at the stars. Even if we're on opposite sides of the world, he'd say, we're still looking at exactly the same stars.

He said it mostly for Gabbi's sake, but it always made both of us feel closer to him.

For a moment I felt like she knew I was there. But how could she?

I stared at my sister's face.

She was frowning.

I froze, hearing someone coming along the path down the side of the house. I ducked down closer to the trunk of the tree.

The footsteps came closer and closer to my position. I hardly dared to breathe. Through a break in the leaves, I could see Rafe walking past, carrying a cup of tea. He paused just beyond where I was hiding. What was he standing there for? Had he heard something? Did he sense my presence? I didn't dare move and run the risk of rustling the leaves.

'Win?' I heard him call. 'Win? Is that you?'

My body tensed up.

My mum's voice called out from the back patio. I could just see her silhouette at the edge of the paving, small and hunched over a table. 'I'm out here.'

Seeing the similarities between Rafe and my dad had me thinking of Ryan Spencer again, and how much I just wanted to ask my mum about it and get a straight answer. A straight explanation.

'I have your cup of tea for you,' Rafe said, walking over and carefully transferring it to my mum's hands. 'Were you out the front a moment ago?'

'No,' she said after a pause. 'How come?'

'I thought I saw someone. Through the window.'

'It was probably just next-door's cat. She's a black cat, sometimes jumps up on the windows, behind the grilles.'

'I'm going to check the grounds,' said Rafe, 'and make sure there's no-one here.'

'It wasn't your fault, you know,' my mum said gently. 'You can't blame yourself for Gabbi's kidnapping. You did everything you could to protect her.'

'One can always do more,' he said, walking off.

He came back to the front of the house and pulled a torch out of his back pocket. What if he shone it up the tree I was hiding in?

'Rafe?' Mum called. Her voice sounded tired, but relieved. 'Look, it is the cat. There she is, just trotting up behind you.'

Rafe turned around again and looked down at the cat.

'So it is,' he said. He shook his head then wandered back inside the house. Mum slowly stood up from the table and followed him, cautiously carrying the cup of tea out in front of her.

Thank you, thank you, *thank you, next-door's cat!*

The black cat stalked away along the path, tail held high. Who said black cats were unlucky?

8:13 pm

Gabbi was still in the window, frowning at the sky.

An idea suddenly came to me.

Gabbi always used to ask me to draw her pictures of cats. Sometimes they were of Snuggles—our old pet cat—and sometimes they were just of any cat or kitten wearing a funny expression. She used to have a few of them stuck around her bedroom mirror. I pulled out the folded leaflets from my backpack, and dug around for a pen.

I quickly scribbled a smiling cartoon cat saying 'Hi!' on the back of one of the leaflets. I folded the whole thing into a paper aeroplane and took aim at her window.

At that moment, Gabbi stood upright and disappeared from the window.

Please don't shut it, I begged silently.

She didn't.

I knew it was a long shot, but I took aim and deftly propelled the paper plane through the air towards the window.

Miraculously, it snuck in perfectly between two of the vertical bars that crossed her window and landed somewhere on the floor inside!

Gabbi would know right away that it was a message from me, while anyone else picking it up would see nothing but a silly cat drawing.

I peered through the window with my binoculars, hoping to see her find it.

She was sitting at her dressing table, combing her hair. She stopped all of a sudden, like she'd seen the reflection of something unusual in the mirror.

My heart pumped with excitement when I saw her jump off her chair and run to the plane on the floor. Her face lit up when she unfolded it like a long-awaited Christmas present.

I wanted so badly to call out—for her to see me—but I knew I couldn't let that happen. I couldn't risk her blowing my cover by accident. I shrank away further into the tree to hide.

She leapt to her feet and ran to the window,

clutching the picture of the cat at her chest. Her eyes searched the yard.

The smile on her face was undeniable.

20 SEPTEMBER

103 days to go . . .

Outside Ryan Spencer's Flat

12:10 am

It was creepy sitting outside Ryan Spencer's window, watching him sleep.

After seeing—hearing—Mum for those few brief moments at Rafe's place, I decided something had to be done. I needed answers. I needed to know who Ryan was. I needed to know who I was. And I needed Mum to know what I knew.

Right now I had my eye on his bus pass, sitting on the floor by his backpack.

I carefully slid my fingers under his window, which was open only a centimetre, and slowly started lifting it. A cold wind blew in and I hoped it wouldn't wake him up.

Soundlessly, I squeezed my body, right leg first, into his room. Once inside I snatched up the bus pass and slipped it into my pocket, but before I could sneak out again, I couldn't help but look for the white toy dog.

It was there on the shelf, just like last time.

I felt mesmerised, frozen to the ground.

Ryan moaned suddenly and turned in his bed, snapping me out of my mindless gaze.

I was back out the window in a flash.

Outside Rafe's House
Surfside Street, Dolphin Point

1:30 am

I scrawled what I wanted to say to Mum on the back of the bus pass, and pushed it into the letterbox.

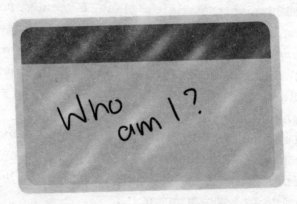

Repro's Lair

3:00 pm

Although I'd been checking every couple of days,

so far I'd received no answer to my email to
Dr Brinsley. I was also impatiently waiting on
word from Boges about the altered air rifle. I
was anxious to move forward with my plan to
get information.

I hadn't heard anything from Sharkey in a
while either. I needed to give him a call.

📱 mission accomplished. items r ready for
collection. w says her place is cool for an hour.
'strictly 4-5pm'. boges.

12 Lesley Street

4:05 pm

'Three hamburgers with the works,' Boges
announced, as he sauntered into Winter's flat.
He passed one to each of us, before letting his
duffel bag fall from his shoulder.

'Thanks Boges,' Winter said. 'Next time it's
my shout.'

'So let's see it!' I said, reaching to unzip his
bag myself.

'Hold on, hold on,' said Boges, brushing my
hands away. He dug into the bag and lifted out
the air rifle, long and sleek, and placed it on
the table. It looked straighter and more polished
than when I'd last seen it. Next to it he placed a
small box.

'You're looking particularly pleased with yourself,' said Winter, pausing in her chewing. 'What's in the box?'

'Custom-designed spyware.' He proudly pushed the box in my direction. 'Take a look.'

'Let me see,' said Winter, pushing in beside me.

I opened it and stared at the contents.

'Wow,' I said. 'This is incredible!'

Gently, I lifted it out. Boges had turned the tiny metallic bug into an insect—a small, dark moth, complete with delta-shaped wings, a tiny head and feelers.

'I used my uncle's old fly-fishing materials to make it,' he explained. 'See this tiny button here?' he said, turning the bug upside down to show me. 'You push it with something small, like the tip of a pencil, to activate it. From that moment on, we'll have roughly twelve hours to listen in to Oriana's conversations—that's if you shoot it into position properly.'

'No pressure,' I said, laughing nervously. 'This is unreal, Boges. I mean, it's *so* unreal that it looks *so real!*'

Winter gently took it from my fingers and turned it around looking at it carefully. 'It's beautiful, and it's perfect that it's a moth. They only have a short life, too, you know. You're amazing,' she said to Boges.

I think Winter's words had made my friend blush.

'I changed my mind about the dart and used this little suction cup instead,' said Boges, showing us a small, rubbery hemisphere at the front of the 'moth'. I've experimented and found that it will hold on to almost any flat surface.' He picked up the air rifle and squinted down the barrel. 'I did some practice shooting using the moth modification—*mothification*, I've been calling it—on ordinary air rifle pellets. I've tried to adjust it, but it's still firing to the right a little. You'll need to correct that when you're aiming. But other than that, it's pretty good over short distances.'

'How short?'

'Ten metres or so.'

'I think that should be OK,' I said slowly, trying to estimate the distance between the window, the tree, and the far wall of Oriana's home office.

'We'll need to find an observation post,' said Boges, 'where I can set up the receiver. It'll have to be somewhere fairly close to our target.'

'Can you hold onto it until we're ready to go?'

'Of course. And you only have one shot at it, remember?'

'How could I forget?' I said, cringing. Nailing my one shot was vital.

6:16 pm

I was striding across the road near the disused railway yards with a warm parcel of fish and chips for Repro when I heard the whoomp, whoomp, whoomp of a helicopter in the sky. I squinted up and my heart sank. It was the police.

Had they seen me?

From not too far away I heard a siren begin to wail.

I bolted over to the three old rusty filing cabinets.

'Repro, it's me,' I hissed, rapping on the middle door. 'Quick! Let me in!'

Behind me the sirens screamed louder; the helicopter hovered closer.

Nothing happened.

I tried again. 'Come on, Repro, don't hold out on me! I think they're on to me!'

I waited for a response but he didn't answer. I couldn't hear any grumbling or muttering.

I knocked harder again. 'Repro, let me in! Please!'

Still nothing. I was beginning to wonder if he was even in there when I heard something that sounded like the scrape of a chair on the floor. The sound of the siren was now ear piercing.

'I can hear you,' I shouted, becoming uneasier by the minute. 'I know you're in there!'

A police car, lights flashing, sped past and continued on its way. I sagged with relief. I looked up to check on the helicopter—it was now a distant glint over the darkening city. This time, it wasn't me they were after.

From behind the filing cabinet wall I heard the chair scraping again. The cops had moved on, but something else was seriously wrong. Every instinct was warning me now. I needed to know my friend was OK.

'Repro, what's going on? Why won't you let me in?'

The sound of something being shifted from behind the wall came as a relief. I pressed against the back of the filing cabinet, and finally it gave way, letting me inside the lair.

In a split second, I saw and understood the situation. I tried to back out, but it was too late! I'd walked into a trap!

Straight ahead of me, Repro was struggling, gagged and tied to his bedhead.

Three-O and another guy jumped out in front of me, grabbed me and threw me to the ground. I tried to fight them off, but Three-O easily wrenched my arm up behind my back, and the two of them hauled me over to a chair near the table.

Repro wailed. I threw him a sideways glance

and saw that he'd just managed to spit the gag out of his mouth.

'They forced their way in behind me, Cal,' he said, panting. 'I was coming back with supplies, and they came from nowhere. Nowhere! They said they'd tell the authorities about my home here! About my collection! They overpowered me—it was two against one. I'm sorry!'

He looked so miserable, struggling in his green suit with the too-short sleeves, and his thin face drooping over his grubby yellow tie. *He* was sorry? I was the one who had brought danger into *his* life.

'Shut up, you old scarecrow,' hissed Three-O's mate. It was Freddy, the guy I'd first encountered in the stormwater drain and then the carpark— the guy who looked like a pirate.

'What do you want?' I shouted at Three-O as he and Freddy started roping me to the chair.

'What do I want?' Three-O sneered. He got right in my face. 'I want to do society a *favour* by aiding the police in the arrest of Callum Ormond.'

Freddy cackled like a hyena.

'There is also the case of this—' Three-O paused and rubbed his fingers together, indicating money. 'I want the reward money and this time I'm gonna get it! There'll be no escaping!

The next people you'll see will be the cops. It's the end of the line for you, buddy,' he said, giving a savage tug to the strong nylon rope that he was tying onto my wrists and ankles.

He stuck his head into my face again. 'You'll regret crossing me.'

I tried to struggle but was completely immobilised.

'Get a move on, Freddy,' Three-O ordered his companion. 'Let's really nail this place up!' Three-O had a hammer and a bag of nails, and Freddy had pieces of timber that he'd ripped up from Repro's tabletop.

That's when I realised that they'd raided Repro's collection. The place had been trashed. Massive guilt weighed down on me as I looked over at my friend, helpless and tied up, watching his home being destroyed.

Freddy smirked at me and then pushed his way through the secret door, disappearing outside. Just before Three-O did the same, he turned to me with an evil grin.

'Thanks for the food,' he said, picking up the parcel of fish and chips from where I'd dropped it in my struggle. Then he turned to Repro. 'Think you're pretty tricky with your secret door, hey? Try getting yourself out of this, Freak Show!'

6:42 pm

Repro and I listened to Three-O and Freddy hammering outside, nailing the timber across the back of the filing cabinet, walling us in. I looked around. The lair was hollowed out of rock, without even a window for escape.

I tussled with my bound wrists, but all the knots held tight. Immobilised like this, all we could do was wait until the cops arrived to arrest me. Repro would be booted out of his home.

'They'll take me away,' said Repro. 'I won't be able to live here any more. They'll lock me up with you. I've avoided them for years, and now . . .'

I'd been feeling really guilty about dragging Repro into this situation so I let him talk. But after he'd been carrying on for a while, I started to panic—every wasted second brought our arrests closer.

'Listen,' I snapped, 'you're not the only one in this mess. You think you have problems? I'll be spending the rest of my life in maximum security!'

'I was only ever trying to help you!' he shouted at me.

Something Dad used to say came into my mind: when you're in a tight spot, don't waste energy whingeing about the situation. Instead, use that energy to find a solution.

'Repro, we have to find a way out of this. Now. For both of our sakes.'

'I've been outwitting those bluecoats for years,' he said, twisting his skinny fingers, trying to get at the knots that tied him. 'It's humiliating to be trussed up and delivered to them like this.'

'So help me think of a way out of here.'

'You heard them hammering and nailing,' he said. 'We'll need a bulldozer to get out of here when they're done.'

'We need to get our hands and feet free, first. We can figure the rest out after that.'

'And we can't even try the emergency tunnel, all tied up like this,' he said.

'Emergency tunnel? What are you talking about?'

'There was a tunnel that I used to use sometimes to get out of here, but I haven't tried it in a long time because of the dangerous rockfalls.'

'Right!' I said, recalling him mentioning it ages ago. I jumped my chair around in a three-point turn to face him. 'If there *is* another way out of here, we have a chance. We have to take the risk!'

'You don't know what you're saying. There's no chance. We're tied up like a pair of Christmas turkeys and the emergency tunnel is practically a death trap.'

'We have to try it!'

Repro stared intensely at his bookcase. 'It's behind there. If you push that aside, you'll find the entrance of a small tunnel that connects to the underground drainage section of that railway line you nearly got creamed on. Remember?'

'How could I ever forget?'

'There was a rockfall when I was in there a while ago, and I was nearly buried alive. Buried alive!'

I shivered. I knew what that fear felt like.

'Anyway,' said Repro, shaking his head, 'it's not even an option. Look at us!' he said, trying unsuccessfully to wriggle his hands and feet free.

'We have to try,' I urged, jumping my chair a little more. I found that if I did it vigorously enough, I could actually inch myself across the floor. If I could get to Repro and turn myself and the chair around, my fingers might be able to undo the knots that were tying him, or his long, supple fingers might be able to undo mine. 'We don't have much time,' I said. 'I'm coming over! You're going to undo my ropes for me.'

I jumped myself across the dusty floor, squeezing past the table until finally I landed myself beside the bed. With immense effort, I jumped the chair around so that I was facing away from him and my bound wrists were behind me, lined up with Repro's fingers.

'Start working your magic,' I ordered. 'Get my hands free, then I'll get yours free. Fast!'

His fingers immediately started scrambling, awkwardly prodding and pulling at the knots behind me.

'Hurry!' I pleaded.

'I'm going as fast as I can! The cavalry will be here any minute now—don't you think I know that? Pipe down and keep still!'

I gritted my teeth, trying to stop myself from saying any more. Sweat was running down my forehead and stinging my eyes.

'Almost there,' he said as I felt the ropes on my hands loosening.

I twisted my hands, squeezed my fingers together, trying to make them as compact and narrow as possible.

'I'm free!' I yelled.

'That you are! Now hurry up and free me!'

I leaned down and began working frantically on the ropes at my feet first. The second I had them out, I jumped up and started pulling at the ropes around Repro's hands and the bedhead.

When we were both finally free, Repro threw the ropes to the floor and jumped up, then almost fell over. 'I'll have to get the circulation back,' he said, stomping his feet on the floor, dancing around like a tall, skinny leprechaun.

'Quit prancing around! Let's get out of here!'

A lot of time had passed since Three-O and Freddy had barricaded us in, and I was feeling nervous, thinking I could hear the helicopter back again.

I started shoving the bookshelf aside, and Repro skipped over to help me.

Outside, it sounded like vehicles were screeching and skidding to a halt. Then came the sounds of thudding feet. I imagined riot police being ordered into position.

'The cops are already here!' I yelled. 'They'll be bashing the door down in seconds! Let's go, let's go!'

Repro started staring up at the ceiling, peering into a dark cavity.

'What are you doing?' I shouted. 'Help me with this!'

He ignored me and kept on staring up above the secret filing cabinet entrance, like he was trying to work something out. He nodded his head and rubbed his hands together.

'Repro, what are you doing? Stop wasting time! We have to get out of here!'

Finally he snapped out of it and helped me wrench the bookshelf aside, sending tiny boxes and bottles flying, crashing and shattering on the floor. A jar of glass eyes smashed to the ground, and all the coloured eyeballs rolled around, staring up at us.

A gaping hole, about the size of an old-fashioned fireplace, was now exposed, leading into blackness.

'The collection!' cried Repro as he watched his treasures scattering. 'All these years of gathering, down the drain!'

He picked up a sack and ran around, trying to stash things from his collection into it.

'We don't have time for that, Repro! Grab the torch,' I yelled.

But he wouldn't stop.

'Where is it? Where is she?' he wailed, searching frantically through the mess on the floor. 'I can't go without her!'

'Who? What are you talking about? Let's go!'

'Aha!' he cried triumphantly. 'Here she is!'

He raced over to join me, clutching the softly tinted portrait of his mother. He shoved it into his shirt pocket.

'They're almost through!' I shouted over the thuds at the door. Repro had reinforced the backs of the cabinet doors, but I knew they couldn't hold out much longer against the onslaught of the sledgehammers, or whatever they were using to break their way in.

Repro snatched up a torch from where it was rolling on the ground, and clutching his sack of possessions, scrambled into the emergency tunnel. I followed him, backpack behind me, crawling quickly, grazing my knees on the way.

The sound of splintering and shattering broke through the air as the back wall of the filing cabinet started to give way. I raced after Repro through the narrow space, following his outline and the narrow beams of torchlight ahead of him.

Stones and rocks rattled past me, one hitting me painfully on the head. All of a sudden I collided with Repro's backside.

'Hold up!' he said.

The yells and shouts of our pursuers echoed from behind us.

'What is it?' I asked, panic-stricken. 'Have we already came to a block? We're not even twenty metres in!'

Repro was reaching into a hole in the roof of the small tunnel we were in. He had a rope handle looped around his hand.

'What are you doing?' I asked, urgently. 'We have to keep moving!'

'Survival Falls,' he whispered back in the same urgent tone. 'I set this up ages ago when I planned on this being a more reliable thorough-fare. Let's see if it lives up to its name!'

I didn't have a clue what he was talking about. All I was thinking about was the cops closing in on us.

Repro suddenly tugged on the rope, with a determined look in his eyes.

At first there was a loud, creaking noise, coming from behind us.

I looked at Repro, confused. He nodded, a barely visible grin appearing on his face.

'Three, two, one!' he counted before a wild rumbling and crashing thundered into our ears!

I started freaking out, thinking the avalanche meant we were doomed—about to be buried alive—but we were OK, aside from a cloud of dust in the air.

Then I saw Repro's face.

He was beaming!

'It worked!' he shouted.

By tugging on the rope looped around his hand, he had released a huge pile of pent-up rocks, held in place above the lair opening by some sort of timber loft. That was what he'd been staring at earlier!

'They have no chance of getting through now!' he cheered.

Survival Falls had worked!

'Awesome, Repro,' I said as I looked through the slowly settling dust to the rocky mountain barricade behind us. The filing cabinet entrance was now completely blocked.

His satisfied look soon vanished. 'We still have to get through the rest of this, my boy,' he said, 'and it's not going to be pretty.'

As if in response to his words, another rumble, this time further ahead in the tunnel, shook the ground we were crawling on.

I gasped, my throat filled with grit.

'I warned you,' said Repro. 'This tunnel is unstable. But now we have no choice but to keep going.'

8:15 pm

We continued crawling through the narrow cutting. Repro grunted ahead.

Another rumble shook us. More stones fell on us.

'Move as quickly as you can,' came Repro's muffled voice. 'That sounds like the beginning of another rockfall.'

I scrambled along faster to keep up with him. I didn't care that rocks were cutting and bruising my hands and knees. I just kept following Repro, hoping that any serious rockfall would hold off until we'd reached a safe spot.

8:32 pm

We'd been crawling for what felt like an hour, but was probably only about ten or fifteen minutes, when a loud grinding and rumbling started. The earth was growling, shaking under my hands and knees.

My heart stopped.

Something hit me hard.

8:40 pm

When I opened my eyes again I realised something heavy was pressing on me. My face was flattened to the ground and it was almost impossible to turn my head. I could see a splinter of light through some cracks and wondered where I was for a few seconds.

Nearby, I could hear someone moaning. I tried again to move, but couldn't. Repro and I had been caught in a rockfall that was pinning us to the ground. The light I could see was the beam of the torch, which was also trapped somewhere in the rubble.

'Repro?' I called. 'Are you OK?'

I could hear the rattling of loose stones as he tried to move.

'Repro?' I called again. 'Can you move?'

'A bit,' came his voice, strained and weak.

Again came the rattle and rumble of loose

stones and a lot of huffing and puffing.

'There's a rock trapping my left leg. I'm just trying to—,' he paused, heaving, '—to lift it off.' He grunted as he forced the rock from his body. 'There,' he said, panting, 'it's off. I'm free now.'

'I think I need you to lift some rocks off me. I'm afraid to move,' I admitted, fearful that too much movement on my part could dislodge another avalanche that would completely bury me.

I saw the torchlight swing around as Repro grabbed it, lighting up the narrow black tomb in which we were imprisoned. Dust filled the air and the stench of dampness filled my nostrils. From far away came the distant shuddering of a train.

Repro swore loudly.

'What is it?' I asked.

He swore again.

'Just get me out of here! All you need to do is move a few rocks off me. OK?'

'Whatever you do *just don't move!*'

The panic in his voice worried me. 'What's wrong?'

'Do you remember a game called "Pick-up Sticks"? Where you had to shake these long, thin plastic sticks onto the floor and then start picking them up, one by one, without dislodging any of the others?'

'Please, just get to your point,' I begged.

'I'm trying to explain it,' said Repro, in a hurt voice. 'You see, if I start moving the rocks that are on top of you, even though they're quite small, some of them are supporting a great big boulder that's just balancing on the pointy end of another rock. If I make one wrong move that huge boulder will fall and . . . Let's just say you don't want to know what would happen next.'

I didn't dare move. I held my breath, suddenly intensely aware of the pain and the pressure of the weight that was on my body.

Repro slowly began pulling at stones. I could just see him out of the corner of my eye—he'd carefully remove one from the mass on top of me, and then place it behind him. I could hear him cracking his fingers and muttering to himself about danger and rockfalls and pesky kids who brought nothing but trouble into his quiet little life, in between mournful laments about losing his collection. 'Don't move,' he kept repeating.

I remained silent, too scared to even move my mouth.

'Patience, patience,' he panted, continuing his delicate work. The pressure on one of my legs eased. 'We can't send you back to your mother all battered and bruised.'

'My mother?' I whispered. 'What made you say that?'

'I was thinking of mine, I suppose,' he said, sadly. 'Did I tell you that I broke her heart? I went off the rails, acting like a complete hooligan. Didn't care what I was doing to her. Or to Dad. By the time I'd cleaned up my act, and made a new beginning, I'd lost touch with her. She'd given up on me.'

'Do you think you'll ever see her again?' I asked, carefully, feeling tears sting the back of my eyes as I thought of my lost family, my lost home.

'She wouldn't want to know me,' he said sadly.

Repro lifted another rock, freeing my left arm and left side.

'This is the tricky bit,' he said, sitting back and studying the remaining rock pile.

'I think I'm going numb,' I said.

8:57 pm

'I've worked out the engineering of this last obstacle,' said Repro. 'I'm going to start pulling the higher rocks away and then when I come to the big balancing one, I'll have to lie on my back and use my legs to push it—hard—behind you. If you roll to the side and pull your legs up at the same time, I'm hoping that it will hit the ground back there, missing you.'

I lay there helpless, still unable to move, as Repro picked away at the high rocks.

I heard Repro shoving himself around in the narrow confines of the low tunnel until he was in the best position to use the full force of his body to shift the big stone.

'OK, my boy. I'm about to give this rock everything I have in the opposite direction from you. But you can never predict these sorts of things. I'm going to count to three and on the count of three, I'll rock, you roll. Got it?'

'Got it,' I said, my body tensing with anticipation. I hoped both of my legs would obey me, once the pressure was off them.

He sat back, legs up, ready to kick. 'Right, here goes! One, two, three!'

The weight lifted and with all the strength I could muster I rolled over, snapping my legs up tight.

The huge rock crashed down, just missing my feet. It landed with a massive thud, the shock sending a cluster of smaller rocks tumbling down on top of both of us.

But I was free! We'd both made it!

9:35 pm

We crawled along the dark, crumbly passage until finally we were hauling ourselves through a square-cut hole into a water collection area under the railway line. I looked at the drain cover above us and heard the roaring of a train rattling over the top of it. That was where Repro had saved me the first time.

'If you keep going through the tunnel over there,' he said, 'you'll end up in the park about half a kilometre from here. The opening is well hidden with bushes and shrubs. You should be OK emerging there. Should be OK.'

'Thanks Repro,' I said, simultaneously grateful I was alive, but also feeling incredibly guilty about the trouble I'd caused for him. 'Where will you go? What will you do?'

He sat down on the hard cement floor of the pump area. 'I'll have to find another place,' he said sadly, 'and start again. I may venture back to the lair, one day, to see if anything's salvageable. All those musical instruments, my books, my paintings . . .' He kicked at the ground dejectedly. 'What about Mr and Mrs Bones?'

'I'm sorry,' was all I could offer. I couldn't help him. I didn't have a clue where I should go either. 'Is there anything I can do for you?'

'Nah, look, the Reprobate will be just fine,' he said with a wave of his hands. 'He always is. Setbacks will only set you back as far as you allow them. I'll be fine. You, my boy, should get

out of here before someone finds you. Get on your
way. Get back to business. Forget about me.'

21 SEPTEMBER

102 days to go . . .

9:38 am

I'd slept for a few hours in a quiet shed, deep in someone's backyard, and now it was time to move on. It had been hard falling asleep. I couldn't get Repro out of my mind—I was wondering where he was, and what he was doing. Where would he find a place to sleep?

I was also thinking about my double, Ryan Spencer, and how I was going to make contact with him.

As I stood up, trying to make a decision on the direction I'd take, my mobile buzzed. I fished it out of my backpack—a message from Boges.

📱 going to w's this morning. around 11. coming? plan operation moth invasion?

📱 definitely. i'll b there.

12 Lesley Street

11:17 am

'What happened to you?' asked Boges, frowning. 'You look like you've just been flung out of a cyclone!'

Winter poked her head around Boges to get a look at me for herself. Her nose scrunched up in disgust, before a look of concern took over.

I brushed my hands through my hair, sending dust flying, and held out my grazed, bruised arms. 'More like a mining disaster,' I said, before having to explain my catastrophic night at Repro's—from capture through to the collapse.

Boges and Winter both felt as sorry for Repro as I did. They asked me what he was going to do without his lair.

I wished I had an answer.

12:02 pm

I felt a million times better after a hot shower, and when I stepped over to Boges and Winter I saw that they'd sketched up a rough diagram of Oriana's house and grounds. It was spread out over the table and they were both leaning over it, making adjustments here and there, pointing out the best way of approach. I noticed Boges had brought the duffel bag with him.

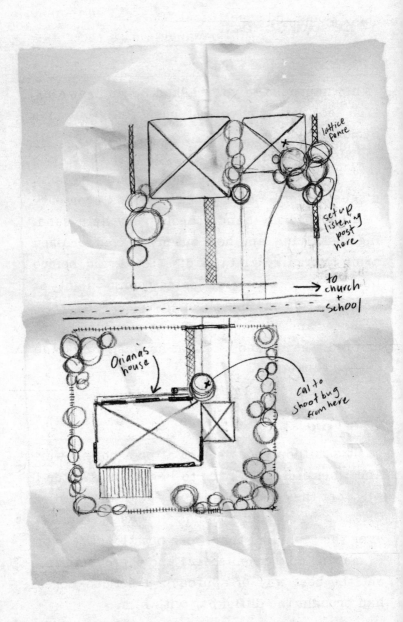

'Come and check it out,' Boges said. He looked at me expectantly. 'We should do it tonight.'

'You're in? Are you sure?'

'You can't do it on your own. Hopefully this tree,' he said, pointing to it on the diagram, 'is big enough for the both of us! Nah, I'm just kidding,' he said. 'I don't need to be *that* close. You're on your own there.' Boges laughed and patted me on the back. 'I'll wait across the road. There's a spot here that I've sussed out,' he said, indicating a house on the diagram that was opposite Oriana's. 'It has a double garage with a roof that looks like the perfect spot for me to set up my listening post. It's well within five hundred metres of our target. We'll meet up there once you've planted the bug. Sorry, the moth.'

I glanced at Winter, who was looking a bit disappointed to be missing out on the action. Keeping two people undercover was going to be tough enough already and it was going to be a hugely risky move. Sumo and Kelvin were still taking turns patrolling the premises.

'So that means once the moth is planted,' I began, 'we'll be staying up there on the roof all night listening?'

'Right,' said Boges, lifting the rifle out of the duffel bag. 'Oriana seems to be most active—

and hopefully talkative—at night. A nocturnal creature. *I can always catch up with my sleep during History. Now let's get some practice!'*

Outside Oriana de la Force's house

8:03 pm

Both dressed in black, Boges and I huddled down in the dark. We were about to go to our separate posts. He pointed out the roof of the garage on the other side of the street where he was planning on hiding. It was perfect—detached from the house it belonged to, next to a scalable lattice fence, and obscured by the thick foliage of an overhanging tree.

Boges was equipped with earphones and a small, specialised FM radio receiver that he'd tuned to pick up the transmission from the bug. He handed me the duffel bag and wished me luck.

The hope of information on the location of the Jewel and the Riddle was making me tense. Not only did I have to nail my one shot, I also had to count on Oriana, or one of her thugs, revealing something crucial to my search in the small, ten- to twelve-hour bracket of eavesdropping the moth would give us. I was nervous with anticipation, but felt excited too.

I also had to remain invisible. There was no way I could let myself get caught on the grounds of Oriana de la Force's house. Especially not with a rifle in my bag. I looked at the dark blue Mercedes parked in the driveway and shuddered.

When the coast was clear, I scaled the tall metal fence and skulked through the shadows up to the pine tree.

8:21 pm

I was about to haul myself up into the lower branches when I heard something. It was the front door, opening. I knew I couldn't be seen from the front entrance but I also knew I wouldn't be safe from view if someone started patrolling through the garden.

When I saw Sumo's figure emerge I knew that was exactly what was happening!

I had studied his routine and knew that he would walk through the front garden and all the way around the side of the house to the back, then up the other side and back towards the main entrance. From there he would check the street before returning inside the house. My mind was working like crazy, trying to decide what to do. I didn't want to start climbing up the tree now in case he heard me, or the unusual movement in the branches caught his eye.

The only thing I could do to avoid detection—and I'd need a whole lot of luck to get away with it—was to crouch beneath the lowest branches and slowly slide myself around the base of the tree trunk, inching along out of sight, as Sumo moved past me.

Sumo strode through the garden, whistling to himself, pausing every now and then to look around before continuing on his way. Stealthily, I started my revolution around the tree. I moved silently, clutching the duffel bag upright and close to me, trying to be as flat and inconspicuous as possible.

From behind the trunk, I heard his footsteps fading as he vanished down the side of the house towards the back garden. I had a small window of opportunity to move. I made a fast decision. Quick as lightning I threw myself up onto the first branches of the pine tree, lugging my bag behind me, and pulled my way up.

I peered down, completely concealed—I hoped—by the bushy pine needles. I was safe. So far.

Moments later, Sumo re-appeared in the front garden, and after a quick sweep of the street, I heard him slam the front door. I exhaled in relief.

By the time I was in position, straddling a branch opposite Oriana's study window, I was drenched in sweat.

I looked straight through the new grille on her open window and watched Oriana herself sitting there, reading something at her desk, her red hair shining in the light. If this evil woman had her way, Gabbi and I would both be dead. I gritted my teeth and tried to focus on what I was here to do.

Clamping the bough tightly with my thighs, I pushed hard against the trunk of the tree, steadying myself as much as possible. Carefully, I lifted the air rifle out of the bag and raised it, practising sighting down its length, cradling the forestock in my left hand, my right forefinger outside the trigger guard. I squinted along the barrel and over the small V-shaped sight at the tip. I aimed it towards the inside wall of the top of the office, at a shadowy corner above her door. Away from ceiling light and the desk lamp this corner provided the perfect spot for my moth to cling unnoticed.

There's no point wasting any more time, I told myself. I opened the air rifle ready to load it and made sure it was steady, wedged between smaller branches, while I lifted the mothified bug out of its box.

My fingers trembled as I held the moth in my hands. I gently activated it by pressing the tiny switch with the tip of a paperclip, and then pressed it into the modified chamber. I relocked the rifle into firing position.

Again, I raised it to eye level and peered along the length of the barrel towards my target.

The moth had to shoot through the grille, through the window, and stick high on the wall in Oriana's office. I tried to stop thinking about how narrow the path was. This was it.

'Here goes,' I whispered.

I took a deep breath, exhaled, and in the space between breaths, I pulled the trigger.

Over the snap of the compressed air crack, I heard a strange 'ding' sound. Ding? What happened?

Oriana lifted her head and looked out the window.

I ducked, shrinking down. Something had gone horribly wrong and Oriana had been alerted! Slowly she stood up and clicked over the red and black tiles to the window.

I'd totally stuffed up the operation. I'd wasted my chance and Boges's money, and now I was about to be sprung!

Oriana's bright, green eyes darted left and right. Her purply-pink lips were pursed tightly in a vicious scowl. The sight of her face sent chills up my spine.

I squashed myself flat along the bough,

praying that I wouldn't be seen, staring straight down at the branch beneath the one I was hugging.

There was something stuck there! The moth!

I didn't dare move to investigate. I waited and waited, wishing that Oriana would decide the noise was nothing and move away from the window. As I stared at the moth, frozen still, I realised what had happened—what I'd done wrong.

The moth had struck the wrought iron of one of the bars and ricocheted back to me, lodging in the branch below. I couldn't believe it. I'd messed up and completely forgotten to consider the slightly crooked aim of the old rifle, but I couldn't believe my good luck! The moth had come right back to me, offering me a second chance! As long as Oriana stopped scanning the view from her window . . .

Incredibly, at that moment, she turned and walked back to her desk.

Straightaway I started climbing down the trunk to reach the moth that was stuck on one of the lower branches. I hoped it wasn't damaged.

'Oops,' I whispered into it as I pulled it off the branch—I figured Boges would be listening in and wondering what happened. 'Messed the first shot up. I'll get it this time, don't worry.'

Back on my platform, I reloaded the rifle, slotting the moth back into the chamber for its second flight. I snapped the air rifle back to its locked and ready-to-fire position.

'Here goes,' I whispered for the second time, angling the rifle slightly off target.

I took a deep breath . . . and fired.

This time I heard nothing but a rush of air. I squinted at my target.

I'd done it! Only a centimetre or two off, the moth was planted firmly on the wall in the corner!

Oriana's head jerked around to the doorway and I panicked. Had she heard it? But luck was on my side again because right then the door swung open—Sumo was there to join her.

He walked into the room and before long they were deep in conversation. Elation ran through me! I'd done it! Now all they needed to do was keep on talking and let the transmitter pick it all up for us!

9:16 pm

I was hanging to get back to the listening post with Boges to see if we could pick something helpful up, but I couldn't rush and take chances now. I slowly and quietly descended from the pine tree and made my way through the dark garden, over the fence and back to the road. I had to duck behind a tree when a car went past, knowing that I would cut a menacing figure, dressed in black, carrying a long duffel bag.

When the coast was clear, I skulked across the road and ran to the double garage, looking around to make sure no-one was in sight as I hauled myself up.

'Dude, I have them!' hissed Boges's voice. He clearly wanted to shout out with excitement, but knew he had to try and keep to a whisper. 'Come and listen! You did it! The moth worked! I'm listening to them talk right now!'

'I almost messed it up—'

'I know! I heard you swear after that "ping-ing" noise!'

'Yeah,' I almost laughed. 'It ricocheted off a bar, but luckily it came right back to me, like a boomerang.'

Boges was tuning his small radio, which was making a low, humming sound.

'Here,' he said, passing me one of the earphones.

Over the humming static was Oriana's unmistakeable voice, loud and clear!

'My client can't possibly appear in court on that date,' she said.

'That's her!' I hissed. 'That's Oriana!'

Boges grinned and nodded knowingly.

'He has a court attendance regarding another matter,' Oriana's voice continued.

'What's she talking about?' I asked.

Boges waved his hand to shush me. 'She's on the phone to someone. Just listen.'

It soon became clear that she was talking to a solicitor about some case she was involved in. Nothing to do with the Ormond Riddle or Jewel.

We heard her footsteps clattering out of the room and then returning—Oriana in her heels—then heard the sound of her chair scraping as she re-seated herself.

Then there was nothing . . .

We'd only been listening in for a matter of minutes, but I glanced over at Boges, impatiently. 'Sumo was in the study earlier,' I said. 'I saw him walk in.'

'Yep, he pretty much just told her the grounds were clear, before whining about one of his shoes being squeaky. She told him to quit his complaining and then he walked out. Hang on—'

The sound of Oriana's heels clicked across the floor again. But this time they didn't come back.

She'd left the room.

10:32 pm

Boges and I had been camped on the roof of the

garage opposite Oriana's for over an hour now, and for most of that time Oriana had *not* been in her study, and we had not picked up any useful information.

I was lying back on the roof, looking up at the night sky, thinking of the smile on Gabbi's face after she'd discovered the drawing I flew to her. Already I wanted to see her again.

Someone else I wanted to see again was Ryan Spencer. Didn't he want to find out about me, too? Or was he afraid of knowing what that would mean?

I wondered how Mum, or Rafe, had reacted on finding the bus pass I'd left for them.

The clicking heels were back. Boges thumped my arm and I sat bolt upright, listening.

'It's me,' said Oriana, sounding as though she were on the phone again. 'Yes. All safely lodged with Zürich Bank. The Riddle, too.'

The Riddle!

Boges and I glared at each other silently—we were both too scared to talk and miss her next words.

'Yes, a safety deposit box,' she said.

Boges looked worried—it was obvious he was unhappy hearing about Zürich Bank. How could we possibly retrieve the Jewel if it was in the possession of a bank?

'I have a cryptographer working on the drawings,' she said.

Oriana had someone trained in breaking codes working for her! Thank goodness Winter had tampered with them!

'Once we have all the information together,' Oriana continued, 'we can move to the next phase. Time is running out and my expert is getting nowhere with the Ormond Riddle. However, he's convinced it's connected to the Tudor Queen . . . Yes . . . Yes . . . Absolutely! What do you think I am? An amateur?' she said before briskly hanging up.

Her chair scraped again and the disappearing clatter of her heels told us she'd left the room, yet again.

After a couple of minutes we heard the sound of a door opening, followed by the sound of taps being turned on and running water.

'She's about to have a bath!' I said to Boges. 'Our transmitting time is slipping away while she soaks!'

Boges was distracted. He silently pointed to Oriana's front yard. I peered through the leaves over the garage to see Sumo checking the grounds again. I strained to see what he had in his hand, but I couldn't make it out. Was it a weapon?

'He's paranoid,' I said, 'and he has reason to be. Maybe he's sensed something going on.'

Sumo stood near the entrance to the driveway and appeared to squint down the road, scanning the street. Surely he couldn't know about us, hiding on the neighbour's garage roof. I froze, scared that he'd see us despite the leaves that surrounded us. This guy was a bodyguard, his job was to know what was in his environment. If he knew what was going on—that we'd bugged his employer—we'd both be dead.

I breathed out again as he turned and walked up the driveway and to the front door. He disappeared inside the house.

Relieved, we turned our attention back to our receiver. Oriana was singing to herself. She sounded horrendous.

'She sounds like she's gargling,' I said.

'More like drowning,' said Boges. 'My uncle's metal grinder sounds better than she does.'

'What if she gets out of the bath and just goes to bed?' I asked with alarm. 'We'll be sitting here all night wearing out our battery listening to her snore!'

'Chill out. She's a busy woman. My bet is she'll be out of that bath pretty quickly. You've seen her here at night—she's always up late.'

He was right. The dreadful warbling continued

and I was about to turn the volume down when I thought I heard Sumo's voice.

'Listen,' I said, prodding Boges. 'Sumo's yelling out something.'

'Hey boss! You upstairs?' came the voice over the radio.

'He's looking for Madame de la Force,' hissed Boges.

The dreadful singing stopped.

'I'm in the bath, Cyril!' Oriana snapped.

Boges and I looked at each other, both thinking the same thing. Cyril? Sumo sure didn't look like a Cyril!

'I suggest you get out of the bath,' Sumo called out, his voice a little clearer, but still muffled. 'We have a problem.'

We heard a swish of water and I imagined Oriana suddenly sitting up in the bath.

'What is it, Cyril? I really don't fancy leaving this tub right now.'

'An unauthorised transmission,' he said firmly. 'Unless you're sitting in the bath transmitting at around 33 megahertz, we have a problem.'

Boges and I looked at each other in horror.

'What on earth are you talking about? I'm not transmitting anything. I'm trying to enjoy a bath,' came Oriana's surly voice.

'I'm just doing what you pay me for.'

There was more splashing and muttering, as well as creaking from what I pictured was a porcelain tub as Oriana stood up to get out.

'Wait in my office,' she called. 'I'll be out in five minutes.'

We heard the sound of the bathwater gurgling down the drain and Oriana moving around.

'Explain yourself Cyril,' she ordered. Her voice was suddenly loud and clear—she must have returned to the office, within close proximity to the bug we'd planted. 'This had better be important.'

'I suspect someone is stealing audio from this house.'

'Stealing audio? From here? That's impossible!'

'I'll rephrase that, then. *Something* is transmitting sound from this house.'

Boges and I had been sprung! We stared at each other, trying to work out how Sumo had stumbled upon our tiny, hidden bug. We were both mentally preparing for a quick getaway.

Oriana let out a fiery string of questions. 'What do you mean—my place is bugged? How is that possible? How do you know this to be true? How could you let this happen?' she demanded.

Sumo was equally furious.

'I was doing a routine security sweep around the premises with my scanner and I picked up the transmission. From this place. Your place. Don't you dare try to tell me I'm not doing my job!'

A scanner? I thought Sumo was clutching his mobile—or a gun—when I'd seen him in the yard earlier.

'This is that repulsive criminal Vulkan Sligo's doing! I'll bet he's behind it!'

'No more names!' Sumo's voice cut across hers. 'The bug!' he reminded her.

'Damn the bug! Everybody knows Vulkan Sligo is a criminal! Can you hear me, Sligo?' she screeched. 'You're not going to get away with this!'

'You'd better keep your mouth shut,' Sumo threatened her.

'Or it's that slimy Sheldrake Rathbone!' Oriana said, dismissing Sumo's warning. 'I couldn't trust that scoundrel as far as I could throw him! If he thinks he—'

We heard a crash as Oriana was suddenly silenced. There was a scuffle—we could hear things crashing to the floor, over the top of some grunting and troubled murmurs.

Boges and I were wide eyed, trying to imagine what was happening. Had Sumo just pounced on Oriana, wrestled her down, hand over her mouth, in an attempt to shut her up?

The scuffle stopped. Now we could hear panting.

Oriana cleared her throat.

'How do you expect me to react,' she finally spoke again, her usually strong voice faltering, 'if I can't rely on you to keep this place clean?'

If only she were talking about housework.

She cleared her throat again.

'You'd better find it then,' she continued. 'Call Kelvin. I want a complete security sweep—from the basement to the roof.'

'Yes,' said Sumo. 'I'll use this. A more refined scanner. Might as well start with your office.'

All of a sudden I noticed Boges packing up his things. 'We'd better get out of here,' he said, the panic clear on his face. 'I'm serious,' he added, pulling out his earpiece. 'Quit listening. We have to go!'

'I'm getting a very strong signal here,' Sumo's voice came through the earphone. 'It's got be up here somewhere, high on the wall.'

'But there's nothing there,' I heard Oriana scoff, 'except for that little moth.' The sound of the chair scraping screeched into my ear.

'You don't mean to tell me that that's the bug!' she cried.

There was a loud crash and the transmission suddenly ceased, shooting a painfully piercing noise directly into my eardrum.

I grabbed the thin cord and ripped it out of my ear.

'He stomped on it!' I said, over the loud ringing in my head.

Boges grabbed up the radio, pulled the two earpieces to him and scrambled to his feet. He swung the duffel bag with the rifle in it over his shoulder. 'Let's go!' he said, before leaping off the roof and sliding down a pipe.

I scrambled off the roof after him, but lost my footing and fell awkwardly all the way to the ground. I grabbed my back in pain.

Boges ran to my side and wrenched me to my feet.

'Come on!' he yelled at me. 'Run!' He seized my arm, hauling me along behind him.

22 SEPTEMBER

101 days to go . . .

12 Lesley Street

12:12 am

Boges threw down his things and crashed on the small patch of grass near the lined-up rubbish bins. We'd ended up downstairs from Winter's place. We were both totally wrecked.

When Boges could finally speak, he sat up and shook his shaven head.

'Zürich Bank . . . Dude, we're stuffed.'

That was not what I wanted to hear.

'You don't know those security accounts at Zürich Bank,' he said before exhaling loudly. 'The vaults are encased in concrete and steel. They're bombproof, fireproof and earthquake proof. Plus they're protected by biometric security. There's no way in.'

'Biometric security?'

'That's right. Fingerprint recognition and a PIN as well.'

Steel and cement. Oriana's fingerprint. Oriana's secret PIN. All impossible obstacles.

Solving the mystery of the Ormond Singularity was out of our reach.

I turned to my friend. 'So what do we do?'

Before Boges had a chance to answer my question, my phone vibrated in my pocket.

'How's it going?' asked Winter. 'Any info yet?'

'We're downstairs,' I admitted, grimly. 'Explain when we come up?'

12:25 am

I sat at Winter's table, dejected. My elation over landing the bug in Oriana's office had been brief—wrecked by the impossible information it had given us shortly after.

Boges had decided against coming up, and instead made his way back home, air rifle in tow.

Winter lifted her head from the table from where she'd flopped after hearing the news about Zürich Bank.

'What about Repro?' she asked, hopefully. 'Can he help?'

'I don't even know where he is,' I said, getting up and walking to the window. 'Now that his hideout has been blown. But I don't think this is the kind of safe he can help us with anyway.'

'OK,' said Winter jumping up from the table.

'Let's think about something else.'

She went to her desk, pulled out a piece of paper from her drawer, and handed it to me.

> * A love whose works must always be kept secret.
>
> AMOR ET SUEVRE TOSJORS CELER
>
> 13th Century poem —middle french
>   poem—La Chastelaine de vergy

'Miss Sparks?' I asked, assuming the new note had come from her tutor.

Winter nodded. 'That's her translation. What do you think it means?'

'Secret love. And the *workings* of that love, also have to be kept secret,' I said, thinking it over in my head as I spoke. 'What if it means secret letters? What if it means the Ormond Riddle? That's completely concealed.'

'I'm beginning to think that you are an intelligent life form after all,' she said, playfully.

'I like that idea. Maybe it's a reference to the Ormond Singularity itself. Look how much trouble Black Tom—or someone—has gone to in order to hide it. All that elaborate double-key code business. You couldn't get more hush-hush than that. In the days of Queen Elizabeth people lost their heads for saying or doing the wrong thing. That's a good enough reason to keep certain things quiet. If only we knew what the certain things were.'

Winter cocked her head to one side. 'Mottos were very popular in medieval times—you know the sort of thing you see on coats of arms? Anyone who was anyone had a motto.'

'But these words have been engraved very carefully *inside* the Ormond Jewel,' I said. 'They're not in full view for everyone to see, like on a coat of arms. They've been kept hidden. For particular eyes only.'

'You're right,' she said, slowly. 'It's the things that are hidden that are really big—really important.' She pulled out another piece of paper and passed it to me. It was a printout from a webpage. 'Read it,' she said, 'and you'll see another side of Black Tom Butler.'

I skim-read the first few paragraphs, but my eyes were drawn to the final one. I looked up at Winter. 'He had twelve illegitimate children?'

She nodded. 'He was a real ladies' man!'

'It's crazy,' I said, 'calling kids illegitimate. Anyone who gets born has a legitimate right to be here.'

Something sparkled in Winter's dark eyes. 'Maybe that's what the motto is referring to!' she cried. 'All the works of love! All the extra kids!'

The sparkle suddenly faded. 'But that couldn't be it,' she said. 'There's nothing secret about them.'

Winter yawned and flicked the kettle on.

'Planning on going back to the car yard?' I asked her, changing the subject.

She looked over at me, her face serious. 'Do you know what I like most about you? I'll tell you,' she said without pausing for an answer. 'It's your determination. I like the way you don't give up. We both have that passion to set things right, no matter what. I'm definitely going back to the car yard. I knew I'd find the car there, and now I have to go back and check over every bit of it, and find out once and for all exactly what happened. No matter what.'

'I'm here to help,' I offered.

'There's something else I have to do, too.'

'And what's that?'

'I need to find my parents' wills. I want to

see their instructions and their signatures for myself. I want to see with my own eyes that they really did leave their estate and most of their money to Vulkan Sligo. See, I keep asking myself . . . what if the will was a forgery? What if Vulkan forged my parents' signatures? He was a trusted manager. He managed their properties, handled their money, all those kinds of things. It wouldn't have been that difficult. Cal, we both know what greed can do to people.'

This changed everything—I hadn't realised how much wealth Sligo had gained from Winter's parents' deaths.

'Do you think he played a part in the accident?' I asked bluntly.

The kettle started whistling. Winter reached into the high cupboard for a couple of tea bags. I hoped she wouldn't ignore my question.

'That's the hypothesis I've been testing out for the last year or so,' she admitted, matter-of-factly. 'That's why I wanted to find the car. I want to see for myself that there was nothing wrong with it. Inside. That nothing had been tampered with. That it really was . . . just an accident. Until I see that everything's in order, I won't be satisfied.'

7:02 am

Biometric security. I woke on Winter's couch with those two words ringing in my ears.

I crept out of the flat to get some fresh air. Overhead, a jet roared through a pale blue sky streaked with silvery clouds. Even though it was early, the city was waking up.

Back inside, I sat on the couch with my phone plugged into its charger, and started searching for information.

It seemed hopeless. Sure, some genius technical people had been able to fool the fingerprint scanner, in one case by making a mould from a fingerprint left on some executive's stress ball— that plasticine-like stuff people squeeze while they're thinking.

It wasn't until I came to a small section on latent fingerprints, and how they could be made visible in a fume cupboard, that I started to see a possibility. But I needed to check it out with Boges.

Finally he answered his phone.

'You want to hack Oriana's fingerprint? What are you going to do? Excuse me, Ms de la Force, but can we please chop off your index finger? Dude, get real.'

'I've been researching it. It can be done,' I

said, 'without her losing any of her digits. It's pretty complicated, but not impossible.'

'OK, even if we can somehow hack her fingerprint, without actually hacking off her finger, have you forgotten the matter of the PIN—the secret number of the safety deposit box?'

'Of course I haven't forgotten that. But one thing at a time. If I can get a good fingerprint from Oriana,' I said, 'on something I can take away with me easily, I can use superglue to create a reaction with the natural oils on the fingerprint.'

'Respect, dude. I didn't realise you were such a scientist.' Boges was quiet for a moment, thinking. 'So this residue leaves a build-up. That means that the patterns in the ridges of the fingerprint are higher than the other parts?'

'Exactly,' I said. 'I can make a print from that. But it's a mirror image. So I have to turn it around again.'

'Like making a negative and then printing a positive from that,' said Boges. 'You make a negative of the fingerprint?'

'Correct. By repeating the exact same process, I'll end up with the right imprint. I hope.'

'Then you attach the film to the top of your finger and fool the scanner?'

'That's the theory,' I said. 'That will give us

a good fingerprint which I can use to access the scanner at the bank. Well, not me actually. I was thinking of Winter. Can't you imagine her wearing a big red wig, purple sunglasses, high heels and a long leopard-skin print scarf?'

'In theory it sounds good . . . but I really don't know if it can be pulled off. How are you going to get her fingerprint?'

'I need to follow her, and I need to borrow your bike again.'

'OK. Look I've gotta go, Mum's calling out to me. Let's figure this out later?'

26 SEPTEMBER

97 days to go . . .

2:00 pm

Boges had found me a place to stay for a few nights, in between staying at Winter's.

I'd been spending my days trailing Oriana on Boges's bike, trying to find information, and trying to come up with an idea on how to get hold of her fingerprint. Whenever she went out in her dark blue Mercedes, I would emerge from my hiding place in the garden across the road, jump on Boges's bike, and follow her, keeping my distance. Once she was on foot it was easier. Her thick, red hair and her swaying way of walking in her high heels made her stand out in almost any crowd. The purple suit and leop-ard-print scarf fluttering in the breeze helped, too. Sometimes she'd go to Estelle's Hair Salon, sometimes to her city office, sometimes on busi-ness lunches with clients, sometimes it was a trip to the shops. And sometimes I lost sight

of her car in seconds, missing my chance alto-
gether.

Another problem was that Sumo was never
very far away.

29 SEPTEMBER

94 days to go . . .

12 Lesley Street

10:12 am

'You're back,' she said, letting me into her flat. I could feel a smile growing on my face, especially at the excitement in her voice. She'd phoned to tell me she had news that couldn't wait. 'Quick, sit down.'

She hopped down, cross-legged on the couch beside me, her computer in her lap. Sparkles in her long, wild hair flashed—something I hadn't seen in a while—and the turquoise eye shadow she was wearing made her dark brown eyes look softer, lighter.

'I have something to show you,' she said. 'Take a look at this.'

I watched her while she pulled up a website and opened it, clicking on images. I leaned closer to see that the screen was filled with thumbnails of Queen Elizabeth the First. Winter enlarged one of them and pushed the laptop in my direction. Her face was flushed with excitement.

It was a portrait of a girl—the Queen—with red-gold hair streaming over her shoulders, wearing a dark blue dress covered in tiny roses. I reckoned she must have been about my age.

Around her neck were several strings of pearls, while pearls also hung from her ears.

But it wasn't the jewellery Winter wanted me to see.

In the crook of the girl's arm, looking up at her with its small, cute, almost human face was a white monkey with a golden collar, holding a tiny golden ball. He was just like the animal Dad had drawn!

'It's the monkey!' I said. 'You found him!'

'Uh-huh,' she said, smiling proudly. 'It's the young Elizabeth,' Winter explained, 'before she became the queen. See—"Portrait of Princess Elizabeth, 1547",' she read.

In her right hand, the princess held a white- and-gold covered book, embroidered with a decorative 'E' while her left hand held an enamelled and jewelled locket. Winter heard my sharp intake of breath as I focused on this—the long white fingers gracefully cradling a locket decorated with a rose, just like the Ormond Jewel.

'Uh-huh,' she said again, nodding. 'It's the same as the reverse side of the Ormond Jewel. A rose. Like the boy is holding in your dad's other drawing.'

'How did you find it?'

'I knew it was familiar, somehow. But I couldn't remember where I'd seen it—the white monkey, I mean. Then it finally came to me. I'd seen it in an art catalogue.

'From time to time one of the great houses belonging to the English nobility has to sell some of its artworks to help pay taxes and upkeep. Sligo's been receiving catalogues from these high-end auctioneers—lately, he's become very interested in art.'

She must have noticed the dubious look on my face. 'Not in art itself,' she said, 'but in its value. Actually, I think he's already "acquired" some valuable paintings.'

'Acquired?'

'Stolen, probably. I called in to see him the other night and all these paintings were being carried in the back. It must have been almost midnight. What sort of people deliver paintings at that hour?'

I couldn't help but feel weird about her being at Sligo's place at that time of night and I tried to work out when it might have been.

Winter continued. 'Anyway, I love looking through the auction catalogues—there are some incredible paintings in there—and I must have seen this one and then forgotten about it. I went back in search of it and read that it came onto the market about a year ago. Until then, hardly anybody knew of its existence.'

I studied the portrait of the girl again. What was she telling us? What was Dad trying to tell me in his drawing of the boy and the rose?

'I wish we had the Jewel here,' I said. 'The locket she's holding in the painting looks the same. The same gold around the edges, the same shape and size.'

'Except that on the reverse side of the Ormond Jewel there's an extra bud. Apart from that, it looks identical. Maybe there was a pair of them. It's pretty exciting! Anyway,' Winter said, looking at the clock, 'want some help collecting Oriana's fingerprint?'

1:25 pm

We tracked Oriana down in a café I'd come to learn was one of her regular haunts. We were looking through the window of a surf shop outside, when Oriana suddenly emerged from the café and headed down the street away from us.

'Mind the bike?' I asked.

'Yep, go after her!'

I'd considered dashing into the café and grabbing the cup she'd been drinking from, but dropped the idea. I had to be sure that I'd get a good fingerprint of her right index finger.

Oriana stepped into a fashion boutique around the corner and I pulled up, watching her through the display of handbags and shoes in the front window. She was wandering around inside, picking up handbags, examining them, and putting them down again. This was my chance.

I walked into the shop, hands in my pockets, trying to go unnoticed. Luckily the sales assistant had focused all of her attention on Oriana. Out of the corner of my eye, I saw Oriana pick up a brown patent leather bag. She gave it a good squeeze while she was opening it, and again when snapping the clasp shut. Perfect, I thought. On the side of that shiny, brown patent leather, there would be a nice fat fingerprint.

The assistant, who'd been hovering around Oriana, pointed out a silver handbag high on a shelf in the corner. The pair moved away, giving me a clear run.

I had my target. With a swift move, and careful not to touch the side of the brown handbag, I snatched it up and bolted from the shop.

As soon as I ran through the security stands

that covered the doorway, the alarm started going off.

I leaped out into the street.

'It's the Psycho Kid,' someone shouted.

I could hear the shopkeeper and Oriana de la Force screaming after me as I raced around the corner and saw Winter jump to her feet.

'Don't touch the side of this!' I yelled, tossing her the patent leather bag. 'It has the print on it—quick! I'm being chased!'

Winter caught it by the handles.

I threw my leg over the bike, preparing to cycle away like crazy, when I looked back and saw Winter's eyes widen with fear.

'Behind you!' she shouted.

But it was too late. Just as I was taking off, someone crash-tackled me from behind and I fell heavily to the ground.

3:20 pm

When the red and black tiles came into focus through my aching eyes, I realised with a sick feeling that I was in big trouble.

As my brain groped its way to consciousness, a voice floated around my head.

'This little grub has been nothing but trouble. Why is he still here?' Oriana's voice screeched. 'There are little more than three months left and I can't make head or tail of what we have so far! The cryptographer is costing me a fortune and he's not getting anywhere! And we still have this,' she said, kicking my foot, 'getting in our way! How hard is it to get rid of a boy?'

I kept still on the floor, wildly trying to think of a way out of my situation. But when I went to move, I realised my hands and feet were tied.

Tied up, two times in one month . . .

Suddenly, I was seized around the neck and dragged to my feet. Oriana had wrapped her leopard-print scarf around my throat and was pulling it tight.

'You're choking me!' I croaked, struggling to free my airways.

'That's the idea!' Oriana screamed, jerking on the scarf harder. I gasped for air. Her furious face was almost the same colour as her hair and she sprayed me with spit as she screamed. 'Here, Kelvin,' she said, releasing me. I fell forward, coughing and spluttering, sucking down air. 'Pat it down. Make sure it's clean.'

She was calling me 'it'!

'I'm going to get rid of you once and for all,' she said, picking me up again after Kelvin had checked me over. She gripped me by my hoodie. 'You're going to go somewhere you'll never, ever return from! You've cost me a fortune! Your interference is finally over—for good!'

With that, she slapped me across the face. I was shaking with fear and my head throbbed even worse. I could barely stand because of the way my feet were tied. 'My friends know where I am,' I bluffed, wondering why she wouldn't just finish the job right then—kill me and be done with it. 'You won't get away with this,' I threatened.

'Oh, I am so scared!' she squealed sarcastically, and then turned on Kelvin.

'You're dumping him in Dingo Bones Valley. Where you disposed of that other bag of . . . bag of *waste*.'

'Dingo Bones Valley? Do I have to? Boss, that's—' Kelvin started to say.

Oriana swung around and slapped him. 'That's exactly where you're dumping him! I don't want to hear any complaints! You're paid to do what I tell you!'

'But boss, how's he expected to—'

'Expected to what?' she snarled. 'Expected to nothing! He's going to be dead when you dump him—well and truly dead—do you hear me? Can you get that through your thick skull?'

'You can't do that!' I said. 'You have everything you want! You've stolen the Jewel and the Riddle. You have my dad's drawings! What else do you want?'

She shoved me towards Kelvin, ignoring my pleas entirely.

'And you'd better be more efficient than those two hopeless fools you hired to do the *swap* with the little girl,' she said to Kelvin. 'I don't want anything like that happening again. If you mess up this time, I'll throttle your other cat. Got it?'

Kelvin muttered something.

'Cyril?' Oriana called out the door of the study.

Next thing I knew, I was being dragged down the stairs by Kelvin and Sumo and out the back of the house where another car, a light grey sedan, was parked beside Oriana's dark blue Mercedes. Sumo opened the boot of the grey car, picked me up with one hand, and shoved me into it. The lid slammed shut and I was thrown into darkness with a sick sense of déjà vu.

'Let me out of here!' I screamed and thrashed. 'You can't do this!'

'What are you going to do, buster? Call the cops?' hissed Sumo's voice.

I lurched sideways in the darkness of the boot as the car started, swung around and took off.

This was the end of the line for me. Dingo Bones Valley was way out in the desert. It was notorious. People said that it got so hot out there, that birds dropped dead out of the sky. It was the sort of area where people were found dead lying near their cars, because they'd broken down and run out of water. Or they'd be found, kilometres away, dead on the track, where they'd collapsed in their useless search for water. Sometimes it was weeks before another car came by. I would never be found. Maybe in years to come, someone—a prospector—might stumble upon my rotted corpse.

In the suffocating heat of the boot, I bumped along, my arms and legs aching from the unnatural position that I was tied in. I blinked in and out of consciousness—barely able to breathe.

11:21 pm

Long hours passed and I started to get cold. As hot as the desert was during the day, it was just as dangerously cold at night. Although the boot ride was horrible, I was begging for it not to end. I didn't want to have to face what was going to greet me outside once we stopped. But, inevitably, the car stopped.

I tried to think, to plan a possible escape. But what could I do? Without the use of my hands and legs, escape was impossible.

A sudden rush of cold air hit me as the boot was opened. Kelvin loomed over me but I couldn't see his expression in the darkness.

'Just leave me here, Kelvin,' I begged, as he hauled me out. He was alone. 'Please. You don't have to kill me. She'll never know.'

His silence was frightening as he threw me on the rough ground. I was barely aware of my surroundings. Ahead of me, I thought I could see a ridge, and above it the starry night sky.

'Just get in the car and drive away,' I said. 'You've done what she told you to do. You don't want my death on your conscience, do you? Kelvin, don't you remember? I saved you when those guys were beating you up outside the casino that night. You can't kill me.'

'I don't owe you anything,' Kelvin muttered.

'I'm not saying you do. But Kelvin, she's a horrible woman. She killed your cat? Why do you keep carrying out her dirty work? I heard the way she talks to you. You deserve better than that, Kelvin.'

He gave me an intense look but said nothing. The night air was cold, but sweat was dripping down his brow like he'd just run a marathon.

'Surely you'd like to be free of her,' I said. 'Work for someone who has some respect for you?'

'I know something that she doesn't know I know, and I could—' he started to say.

'What?' I asked, stalling for time. 'What do you know about her? What could you do?'

'Shut up!' he demanded, his voice hardening again. Something like fire blazed across his eyes. He reached into the car and pulled out a gun.

'Don't do it!' I pleaded.

'I told you to shut up!' he said, aiming the gun at my head. 'Can't you get that through your thick skull?'

I knelt on the ground with the desert sounds rustling around me, and waited for the end. I said goodbye to my mum and Gabbi, and Boges and Winter.

The sound of the shot rang out.

30 SEPTEMBER

93 days to go . . .

Dingo Bones Valley

10:05 am

Blazing heat. Pain. Aching wrists and legs. Thirst. Thirst.

Slowly, I tried to open my eyes. They seemed to be stuck together. I could barely swallow, my mouth was so dry. I was lying face down in the red dust of Dingo Bones Valley. But I was alive.

I spat red dust out of my mouth and rolled over. The blazing sun beat down on me. I tried to sit up and rolled over onto my belly again, away from the light. My eyes ached. They were dry and filled with grit. Scared at what I might find, I slowly put my hand to the right side of my head, where the shot had deafened me. I felt around gently. But there were no wounds, no blood. Then I noticed, in the red dust, a long straight track made by something small and moving fantastically fast. Was that the bullet track?

The shot must have been deflected in some way. Because I seemed to be OK. OK, considering I'd been dumped in the middle of Dingo Bones Valley, tied hand and foot.

What? My hands and feet were free! I crawled to my feet and saw the ropes lying beside me—they looked like they'd been cut through with a knife.

Somebody had freed me. But who? Kelvin?

I looked around in the shrill, desert air. Not a soul in sight. No living thing at all. Just the red dust stretching out in every direction, broken here and there by clumps of dried, white grass.

Without food and water, I was as good as dead. I looked around for shelter, but there was nothing. No shade, nothing. I lay back, defeated.

As I squinted towards the sky, I saw two eagles circling. Were they waiting for me to become weak enough for their attack? I could die lying down, or I could die on my feet, trying to find my way out. The choice was mine.

I climbed to my feet and started walking.

12:00 pm

I realised that there was, in fact, a road. But it was almost impossible to see, because the road looked much the same as everywhere else—red and dusty. I knew that if I was ever going to be found, or if I was ever going to find anyone, I had better stick to this road.

Every slow footstep was painful, every breath scraped through my dry throat. My tongue felt like an old boot and my lips were cracked and parched, splitting painfully at the edges. I pulled my hoodie over my face in an effort to keep out the scorching sun.

I'd been walking for hours. My mouth was getting drier and drier, but I forced myself to keep moving.

The landscape never changed. It was nothing but endless red dust, millions of microscopic crystals twinkling under the searing sun, with the occasional tuft of bleached grass. From time to time, I saw bones. Nothing lived here except the eagles and the crows. Even the dingoes had more sense to go elsewhere.

My feet were swelling up and I could feel blisters on the back of my heels.

My socks were slipping. I sat down and undid my sneakers, pulling them off. As I removed the sock from my left foot, I leaned forward, puzzled. There was something black on my ankle. I tried to focus my dry, bleary eyes. There was something written there.

SDB 291245

Letters? Numbers? I couldn't focus my eyes.

What? Did Oriana de la Force catalogue and number all her victims like this? Who had written this on me? It looked like black ink. I looked at my sock. There was nothing on that except red dust. Nothing had rubbed off. I didn't have enough spit to try wetting it. But it seemed that someone had written these letters and numbers in permanent ink on my skin.

I pulled my socks and shoes back on and kept going.

Before long I heard some kind of noise. At first I thought it was just the roaring in my head. My heart was pumping hard and I imagined my blood turning into toffee as I dehydrated. How long could I go on like this? But the sound persisted. I stopped my dragging footsteps and listened.

It was the sound of an engine! I stared into the west, trying to make out something in the distance, blinded by the sun glaring straight into my eyes.

It was the sound of a car! In the distance I could see a puff of red dust near the horizon. It was a vehicle, and it was coming my way!

I staggered out into its path, waving my arms like a madman.

'Hey! Stop! Over here! Stop!' These were the words I tried to say, but they sounded more like the squawking of a crow.

I tore off my hoodie and tried to wave it.

The vehicle approached me in a cloud of dust.

It was an old ute with a canvas water bag hanging off the bumper bar. I couldn't take my eyes off the water bag. As it approached, I limped and staggered towards it, waving my dusty hands. I hoped I wouldn't frighten who-ever was driving. The truck slowed and finally stopped a few metres away from me. I lurched and stumbled closer.

'Water,' I croaked. 'I need water.'

Slowly, the passenger door opened. I tried to look through the dusty windscreen, but could barely see into the interior of the cabin, although I could make out the head and shoulders of the driver.

I walked around to the passenger side door and peered in. A dusty, wizened man was staring back at me, a battered hat pulled over his sunburnt features, his hands like claws on the steering wheel.

'There's a bottle of water there, sonny,' he said. 'Hop in and help yourself.'

I didn't need a second invitation. I hauled myself into the filthy cabin of the ute, kicking rubbish away, until I finally fell back exhausted on the seat, grabbing the bottle of water that the driver indicated. I ripped the top off and emptied a litre of water into me in about two seconds flat.

'You sure was thirsty, sonny,' cackled the driver, revealing yellow, broken teeth. But to me, just then, the old guy was about the most beautiful thing in the world. 'You here on holiday?'

I looked at him. Was he serious? Who'd come to this barren desert for a holiday?

He threw his head back in a screech of laughter.

'If you want more water, there's a water bag hanging off the front of the vehicle.'

'I need to make a phone call,' I said. Miraculously I still had my phone on me, but it had no signal whatsoever. Plus the battery was about to die.

'Where are you heading?' The driver asked as the truck lurched off again.

'To wherever you're going,' I said. 'Somewhere I can get a feed and maybe a place to rest. After I've called my friends in the city.'

'The name's Stanley. But everyone calls me Snake.'

'Tom,' I said.

'I've been prospecting,' said Snake, 'looking for sapphires. There used to be gold but now there's no water to wash it in anyway so we go after sapphires instead, my partner and me. What's that tattoo on your ankle mean?'

He didn't miss much, I thought, noticing that my sock had slipped down.

'Just some numbers I want to remember,' I said.

'A phone number? In case you get lost?' The old prospector asked before cackling with laughter.

I squirmed uncomfortably in my seat. I was so relieved that I'd been picked up, but this guy's laugh had a nasty edge to it.

'You're very lucky I came along when I did,' he said, as if reading my thoughts. 'Lucky for me, too. Otherwise, you'd have gone to waste out there.'

I flashed a look at him. That was an odd thing to say.

'True,' I agreed. 'No-one could survive out there for very long.'

'Now, ain't that the truth,' said the old prospector, showing his yellow teeth again as he grinned. 'We were looking for Lasseter's Reef when we first came out here. Me and my partner. That was years ago.'

I wondered if Winter had escaped with the leather handbag OK, and whether the fingerprint had held up. I was impatient to call them. 'When will we be there?' I asked. 'Wherever we're going?'

'Not far to go, now. In fact, if you look straight ahead you'll see the township.'

Sure enough, down the track, I could see the roofs and trees of the township. Soon I'd be able to hook up with my friends again. Oriana de la Force hadn't won this round.

As the old car rattled down the main street, I looked around, puzzled. Where was everybody? Maybe it was the shocking heat keeping everybody indoors. But when I looked at the shops that lined the dusty street, they seemed to be boarded up. After the shops, there was a scattering of houses but they too seemed deserted, with broken windows and vines growing out of the chimneys.

'Is this some sort of ghost town?' I asked

Snake, who was hunched over the wheel, trying to avoid the worst of the potholes in the road.

'Not quite,' he said. 'My partner runs the general store.'

I felt a lot of relief at the mention of a general store. I could use the phone, buy something to eat and maybe even find a lift or a bus to get me back to civilisation.

The prospector was parking the truck when I noticed that the scattering of vehicles parked in the street were really old and looked like they'd been abandoned too.

We hopped out of the cabin.

Snake looked at me and must have seen the confusion on my face. 'The gold ran out years ago. The bank closed, the medical clinic closed, the shops started closing because nobody bought anything anymore, even the pub closed. The young folk all left town because there weren't any jobs. And then, after a while, there were just a handful of old people living here.' He put his hands on his hips and cackled his unpleasant laugh again. 'Then they went, too. So now it's just me and Jackson at the general store.'

The store had some timber steps leading up to a dusty verandah, and a couple of dirty windows stacked with bleached-out displays of groceries and hardware. I followed Snake through the flyscreen door. A little bell jingled as we entered, and a dog barked.

'Jacko? You here? We've got a visitor.'

All the stock looked tired and old: stacked up tinned food with rust spots on the top and peeling labels. Everything was covered in grease, grime and dust. I doubted anyone had bought anything in this general store for a long time, thinking the expiry dates must have been dated ten years ago, at least. On the wall behind the counter was a map of the area, curling round the edges and spotted with fly dirt.

I heard the sound of shuffling feet. 'Who's there?' a voice called.

'Who do you think it is? It's me, Snake. I have a young traveller with me.' Snake prodded me sharply in the back.

Jacko stepped out of the shadows. He was a gaunt, bearded man with sharp eyes hidden under bushy eyebrows. At his side stood a huge black dog.

'He looks OK,' grunted Jacko. 'It's a long time since we've had a visitor. Meet Sniffer here. The best nose in the country, ain't you, Sniffer? He can track anyone, any time, through any country.'

The dog growled and stared with his brown eyes as the two old geezers chuckled. I looked from one to the other, unsure.

'Is there a public phone in here?' I asked.

'Of course there is,' said Snake, smirking. 'Over there.' He pointed to an old-fashioned red phone sitting on a shelf. I stepped over to it hesitantly and picked up the handset.

The line was dead. The handset wasn't even connected to the telephone—it had been cut.

'Vandals,' said Jacko, shaking his bearded head.

'They used to be shocking round here,' Snake added. 'But it's pretty good now, isn't it, mate?'

Jacko nodded. 'Pretty good,' he repeated.

'So what about the phone?' I asked. 'Do either of you have a phone I could please use?'

'You could,' Jacko replied, pulling a mobile phone out of his pocket.

'I'd pay you for the cost of the call,' I offered.

'It would cost you a lot,' Jacko said, gripping the mobile in his leathery hand.

The mean old storekeeper held the power. I wasn't in the mood for games. Not after everything I'd been through.

'Whatever it costs,' I said. 'I have to make a call.'

Jacko looked at Snake and they both laughed.

'OK, then,' said Jacko. 'Do you have any idea how much a telecommunications tower costs?'

I looked at him, confused. He switched on the phone and handed it to me. 'No signal,' I read. I waved it around but nothing changed.

'You mean this is a dead spot?'

The pair laughed disturbingly again. 'You got it, boy!' said Snake. 'You got it in one.'

Here I was, stuck in the middle of nowhere, with two complete weirdos. What in the world was I going to do?

The big black dog shook his head, making the metal tags on his collar jingle.

'Is there anywhere else I can go to make a call?'

The pair stared at me blankly.

'But I have to get back to the city! There are things I have to do! Is there a bus? Do either of you ever drive to the city?'

'Sure,' said Snake. 'I went to the city in . . . '96. Or was it '97? Do you remember Jacko?'

'What about public transport?' I asked, increasingly frustrated with every word they spoke.

I was aware that both men were looking at each other strangely. Something was happening between them that I didn't understand. Like they were communicating without words. Then Jacko spoke.

'Sure,' he said. 'There's that bus that comes through in the morning, isn't there, Snake?'

'That's right. Nice, solid bus in the morning. Only about a fifteen or twenty minute walk from here to the highway. Have you back in the city in seven or eight hours.'

Who were these people and what kind of general store were they running? It was obvious no customers had been here for years. Everything was festooned with cobwebs and the dust on the floor showed no footprints but our own. I wanted to get out. But I knew I had to make it to the highway and wait for the bus.

I moved closer to the map, studying it, analysing the scale. It showed Dingo Bones Valley township and a number of other small townships connected by a single road. That must have been the road the bus would take.

I started walking out of the store. Snake called after me. 'Where are you going?'

'To the highway,' I said.

'Are you crazy? Nobody walks around in the middle of the day here. You don't have any water or any food, and the bus ain't coming till tomorrow. You'd be crazy to go now.'

'And look at yer,' said Jacko. 'Ain't you a sight for sore eyes! You'd be much better off resting for a while then setting off in the cool of the early morning.'

I looked down at my feet, imagining the

multitude of blisters I'd gained. I was exhausted, hungry and still thirsty. They were right.

'There's the boarding house across the road,' said Snake. 'That's where I camp. There are plenty of rooms. Check it out and take your pick. Tell you what. I'll even share my beans with you.'

'Here,' said Jacko, throwing a tin of beans to his mate. 'My shout. And here,' he added, throwing me a water canister. 'You'll need that.'

I turned to go, aware of their eyes on my back. I heard the dog's claws clicking on the dusty floorboards. He followed me out to the verandah.

'Good dog,' I said to him nervously. I was relieved he sat down while I walked away.

3:36 pm

The boarding house reminded me of the St Johns Street dump I'd camped in a while back. The grounds were nothing but dust and prickles, the timber of the upstairs verandah sagged, and the front door hung crookedly on its rusting hinges. I stepped inside and was grateful to find that it was much cooler out of the sun and the heat of the day.

I went up the creaking staircase and walked along the top landing, passing several rooms without doors. Inside the rooms were small cob-web-covered beds and cupboards.

At the end of the hall I found one room that looked a little cleaner than the others, apart from a pile of stuff in the old fireplace. I ignored the bad smell, knowing that I wouldn't be here long enough for it to bother me.

I carefully pulled my sneakers off. The mysterious letters and numbers on my ankle worried me. What did they mean? I decided it could only have been Kelvin who put them there. But why had he done it? I was too exhausted to think. I leaned back on the bed and fell asleep.

10:09 pm

I woke up shivering. It was a cold night, the opposite of what the day had been like. I pulled the crusty blanket off the bed and draped it over me. I noticed that there was half a tin of beans on the small table next to the bed—Snake must have brought it in for me.

The sound of scratching pricked my ears. I froze, trying to peer into the darkness.

Rats. There were dozens of rats squeaking and scuttling around. They were too close. I could hear them rustling and fighting in the rubbish piled up in the old fireplace. The thought of rats running over my sleeping figure made me sick.

I'd slept in a stormwater drain with fewer rodents.

All of a sudden the tin of beans went flying, spilling on the floor. The rats went crazy. I moved back to the furthest corner of the bed. I couldn't wait to get out of this place.

Despite my tiredness, I put my sneakers back on over the strange indelible message written on my skin, and prepared to leave. I looked out the broken window. High above, dark clouds scudded past the moon, hiding its light. I hoped the clouds would clear because I needed moonlight to help me travel to the main road. Hoisting my backpack up onto my shoulders, I crept to the landing.

I could hear sounds from downstairs, the old prospector moving around. I'd have to wait until he went to sleep. I didn't want him knowing that I was leaving. There was something about him that was very, very . . . disturbing.

I'd heard about prospectors going crazy out in the desert, talking to themselves and seeing things that weren't there, and I wondered if Snake and Jacko had been affected. I looked around for something to use as a weapon—I wasn't even sure why, but the atmosphere in this broken-down boarding house had spooked me. I tried to put the scurrying rats out of my mind and looked over the rubbish near the fireplace. I saw something long and white, and I picked it up and looked at it in the pale moonlight.

It was a bone.

Was it human? I didn't intend to stay around to find out.

One foot at a time, testing my weight on every step, I crept down the dodgy staircase. A couple of times I froze when the stair creaked, but nothing happened, and after a few moments I continued until I was safe at the bottom. Flickering candlelight was coming from a room nearby which I imagined was the kitchen, and inside it, Snake was moving around. I could hear what sounded like heavy coins or something being dropped into a tin box. Was he counting his money like some old miser, at this hour?

I'd need to be very cautious getting past the door without him seeing me.

I paused for a second, just beyond the half-closed kitchen door, when I heard him speaking.

Was Jacko there too? I was puzzled and peered in. Back turned away from me, Snake was talking on a mobile! They lied to me about the phones!

'He's sound asleep right now,' Snake was saying. 'Hasn't any idea we're onto him. Just thinks we're a couple of crazy old moonshiners.' He gave a wheezy chuckle. 'Crazy I might be, but I know reward money when I see it walking around! I'll tie him up now and sit on him till the cops arrive.'

Right at that moment, the door I was pressing against creaked open and Snake spun round to see me staring at him. A thick coil of rope sat on his lap.

The prospector and I eyeballed each other for a shocked split second. Then he sprang at me, raising his arms, the rope stretched between his hands.

I charged at him and he staggered backwards, then we both crashed into the kitchen table. He was amazingly strong and wiry and I fought hard to hold him down.

Struggling, trying to get up, I grabbed the kitchen table, but I only succeeded in pulling it down. It collapsed and splintered, crashing down.

Flying off in all directions from the tabletop, a heavy shower of rocks bounced off me.

Huh? *A shower of gold?*

Gold! Nuggets bounced off my shoulders, covering the old prospector's upturned face, skidding around the floor, falling into his open mouth, filling the pits of his eyes.

He thrashed around, trying to rid himself of the golden lumps, spitting them out of his mouth, shaking them from his face. I fought him as hard as I could as I sensed him getting weaker.

But then his hand flew to his belt as fast as the snake he was nicknamed for and I saw the glint of a long, slender skinning knife in his hand.

There was no way I was letting him use that on me!

I fought back with all my strength, grabbing his knife-hand around the wrist, crushing it as hard as I could. He howled, dropping the knife, sending it flying out of my reach.

Any moment Jacko would arrive and I'd be overpowered.

Still straddling the heaving prospector, I leaned forward as far as I dared without letting my body weight lift off him. My scrabbling fingers connected with the knife.

Stretching as far as I could, and risking losing my hold on Snake, my fingers closed around the knife. I snatched it up, swung it back, close to his nose.

He went limp immediately; looking at the knife cross-eyed, then up at me with his desert-reddened eyes.

'You can always count on the kindness of strangers,' he said with an evil smirk.

'That's enough!' I said. 'I'm going to stand up and leave this place, and you'd better not come after me.'

Without taking my eyes off him, I felt around on the floor nearby with my free hand, and gathered up as many nuggets as I could, before stuffing them into my pockets.

I jumped up and ran out the door. His voice thundered after me.

'You can run but you can't hide! Sniffer will get you wherever you are! Me, Jacko, Sniffer and me sawn-off shotgun! We're all gonna come and get ya!'

I ran through the black desert, never wanting to stop. Dead or alive, they were determined to get me.

A quick glance behind me revealed torches flashing, slicing through the dark.

I heard Sniffer barking and the voices of the two bounty-hunting prospectors, stalking me, hungry for my blood.